And Then She Fell

Dreena Collins

FIRST EDITION

ISBN: 978-1-7396126-2-7

Book Cover Design: Dreena Collins

Illegitimi non carborundum.

Chapter 1

From close by came the sound of young people shouting joyously. Free. Their splashing enmeshed with the beat of the music. I recalled the pool with its faded, steep slides. A swim-up bar.

I had left it much later in the trip than I had planned, this visit back to The Palace Hotel. I was not so brave, after all.

As I walked up the slope towards the Reception, my stomach writhed, teeth clamped together, and all those other pangs and sensations in my flesh, my bones, came back in the places where they had sat the year before. When it happened.

Extraordinary.

The doors closed behind me, and the ferocious air-conditioning hit my skin. The lobby smelt salted and clean, just as it had last time. It was all as it had been.

The receptionist was new, however, and continued on the computer as I approached. She held one finger up to show me she knew I was there but didn't make eye contact. I wanted to scream at her. Shriek. But then she lifted her head – curly, dark – and beamed.

"Hello, madam. How can I help you?"

She spoke flawless English, with hardly an accent.

"My name is Catherine Keely," I said. "My daughter died here last year."

***

He was still tucking in his shirt at the back as he came through the door behind the Reception desk. I would recognise Alexander Demetriou anywhere, though his hair was shorter, less fashionable. Last year it had been spiked with gel or wax. Now it was drooping on his brow, and he looked harassed, tired. Perhaps he had been off duty or asleep.

"Mrs Keely," he said.

He put out his hand to me. It was limp, cool, and slightly damp. I placed mine in his, then gave it a firm shake.

"Ms.," I replied.

He gave a tight smile and curled his fingers together, clenching and unclenching them a couple of times as his hand fell back by his side.

"I did tell them not to bother you," I said, "I just wanted to let someone know I was on the premises."

"I will accompany you," he replied. It was not an offer.

We walked through the small shop and across the buffet restaurant, where staff cleared the remains of lunch as others reset the tables for dinner. They ballroom danced around each other effortlessly. The warm smell of recently finished food was in the air – meaty, sweet. The décor was filled with brown tiles of varying patterns, some cracked and uneven – but it was clean, orderly, and bright.

"You seem busy," I commented. "That's good."

I threw the comment away into the flower beds flatly. Didn't mean it.

"We have worked very hard, Ms Keely. We have made many changes."

I had seen no changes so far – but I said nothing.

He walked two steps ahead of me on the fractured path. He hadn't asked where I wanted to go. I kept my eyes on the ground: spotted pink petals on the floor; a discarded bottle of lager, pocked with ants; a small, dusty lizard scurried into the bushes.

Alexander stopped.

"You will see our new fences," he said, "Very safe."

The word 'safe' formed and hovered in the air. It stayed near him. Did not quite reach me. I looked up.

Your block had been repainted a dusky pink. On each balcony, a white railing was now bolted on, raising the height of the wall by forty or fifty centimetres. Armoured. My eyes searched for your room, scanning up the building, desperate, seeking and yet not wanting to see it. The railing that should have been there for you.

The sun was in my eyes: they prickled, hot and dry. I stumbled backwards as I craned my neck and winced. Confidently, Alexander took my upper arm and moved me up the path, turning me around so that the sun was to the side. I took a moment. Then I looked again.

For some reason, I expected to see someone there. Foolish, really. But it was empty and looked the same as all the others.

"We have signs, too. See?"

He pointed to a small white sign tacked to the wall by the entrance of the block. In English, it warned the occupants in blue upper-case writing that leaning over the balcony was hazardous. Presumably, the Greek guests did not need to be told.

I looked around for further signs: beside and behind me. They were near every entrance, though the top letters on the sign in Block D were already overcrowded by a large, virulent rosemary bush. Alexander followed my gaze and without dropping his tight, fixed grin, he took a few steps over to it: snapping the top of the bush away without comment, then striding back, light on his toes. The distinctive scent of the herb followed him.

"They are also in the rooms, and we –"

He looked at me mid-sentence and realised he had said enough. I was hanging, suspended, taut by a thread, and everything he said simply cut away, leaving me spinning. I started to walk back. He followed. We did not speak.

At the Reception, he stopped and put his hand out again, this time with more confidence and a genuine smile. But this was not why I was here.

"Actually, I'm not leaving yet," I said. "I was hoping to speak to some bar or restaurant staff. If there are any here, who worked last summer, as well?"

Flagrant irritation covered his face.

"Why?" he asked.

"Because I have some questions," I answered, unperturbed. "Just a couple of things that might help me to understand."

Could I ever understand? But I needed this. Needed to try.

"They have been asked these questions many, many times before."

"Yes, I'm sure. But not by her mother," I said.

***

Losing a child is a catastrophic experience. It did not matter that you – my darling girl— were 26 when you died. The pain was different, no doubt, though as severe. I am certain.

When you were a baby, I saw you as a fragile chick. A nestling who might stop breathing if I looked away for too long. I lived in a state of terror, amplified a hundred times over by my exhaustion. This is the world of new motherhood. You were an appendage, a new, brittle thing who might snap at the slightest touch or lack of it. I needed you near and to check on you a thousand times a day.

As an adult, I had different fears. I lived with a lurking dread that you might fall foul of someone else's malice or stupidity, as I was no longer close by to help. I feared you would be burnt, bruised, cut. Caught in a fire or a lightning strike. Smashed in a car accident, arrested for no good reason. Brokenhearted. We were still like concentric circles. You were at the heart of me. Focal. Vital.

Sometimes, as you grew up, I would be caught by a morbid fear if you were late returning home or didn't return my call. Something terrible must have befallen you. Some horrific incident or attack. I would hear an ambulance and imagine it must be for you. Think my luck was out. I was losing you.

I knew I could not live without you.

And little did I know, my fears were not so irrational after all. You were going to leave me too soon.

In the days that followed the news, I felt distorted, physically out of my shape, bursting outside of myself, those patterns gone. My emotions did not obey the curves of my own body anymore. I was exploding in heaps and sobs; porous; moving beyond my own perimeters. A brutal mess. And people could not bear to look at me, to see the oozing chaos of me and my pain.

The rooftop bar, here, at my own hotel, was at the edge of a small, modern pool. Everything was tasteful, illuminated, up-lit, rippling, soft. A contrast to The Palace Hotel, with its bright lights and brash sounds. The evening air was warm, vaguely scented. My scarf was lifted and pulled away from my bare shoulders by the breeze; I resisted the itch to lift it to cover my back again. Some days, I was conscious that people might think a 57-year-old woman was too old for a tattoo. This was not one of those days.

Healthy, squat palm trees in heavy pots rustled but stayed put.

I could not wholly appreciate the beauty, the serenity of this place, but there was one benefit of coming back to Crete: I could avoid the discomfort, and disdain of others. Judgement that I was not further along in the journey of my grief. I needed something concrete. Tangible.

I still felt it as a raw, searing thing. One year on. Several times an hour, I thought of you, my lost girl, and it distorted me again each time. The turmoil came back, instinctively, primeval and pure. I could not settle into the quiet, sad shape that they wanted me to inhabit. I was not resolved and bleak. Why should I be? Part of me was still fighting against the story of your death. And I wasn't allowed to voice that, never could, because to everyone else that meant I was in denial. I was not: nothing could bring you back. You were gone. Lost. I accepted that.

But there were question marks, holes, and queries over so many details of your death.

And I was still seeking the answers.

"You enjoyed your trip, Miss Catherine, yes?" Nicholas asked as he cleared my wine glass and took away the remains of the tiny, bitter black olives.

Specks of broken serviette dotted the table like red ants. I looked down at the torn paper in my hand.

"Crete is lovely," I said.

He paused.

"I think this has not been the holiday you hoped for," he said.

I suspected he was referring to the weather, patchy as it was, or perhaps my neighbours in the hotel, who had caused issues the night before, loudly attempting a shortcut back to the resort across a field of courgette plants.

"Something like that," I said with a smile.

"And now I will give you a drink," he declared, "On the house."

I smiled more broadly. A final toast to you.

"That would be lovely."

I turned back towards the small segment of sunset that I could see between the flat roofs - terracotta, white - and the steep, craggy mountains to the right. There were crickets; there was mint, sage and marjoram. I wondered if you smelt the same smells and saw the same sunset when you were here.

Nicholas brought me a small bottle of sparkling wine and a fresh glass, frosty, clouded. I picked up the drink, tilted my raised glass towards the sunset and took a deep swig. The bubbles felt raw and harsh against my throat. The wine was cold and strong.

I closed my eyes and tried to imagine you here: to inhabit the space you occupied, to picture you again – but happy, free, laughing – to walk within your story. I could feel you, almost, yes, and I wanted to pull you in and hold you tight and wrench you inside and hold on to you. Hold on.

I had hoped this trip might help fill in the little gaps, the fissures in the story. And then I could tape things together and construct an image of you. Delicate, buckled, and fragile as handmade paper. As you were. Then I could tell your story – your real story – and show all the people who thought they knew you now, who thought they could judge you, that they had the wrong picture. An impersonation. A parody.

Only I knew you.

I had never believed the lies, the insinuations.

But it was the last night of the trip, and I was no closer to finding the truth. And really, why would I be? All the key players were at home, not here, in Crete, another world away. Your friends. Jessica. Sebastien.

Daniel.

What happened, Susie, my little girl? What happened to you that night?

She tried to shut the door, but he had a flip-flopped foot, a hand, an elbow in the room. She could see the bridge of his nose. Filaments of bristle on his upper lip. There was the sour tang of lager.

Again, she pushed against the door edge. His fingers crunched like eggshells: crumpled. But he did not stop; continued to lunge and thrust.

She had to give up.

She leapt away from the door, taking two steps further into the hotel room as she turned, twisting in a fractured pirouette.

Her bare feet skidded on the tiles as they raced towards the balcony. The door behind gaped then crashed against the wall; she heard it, didn't dare look back – don't look back – as she yanked the sliding doors open enough to squeeze through.

She was on the other side. She had one hand pounding on metal and glass, pushing, sliding the door - the other seeking the latch to lock it behind her.

But he was there. His hands were there. A forearm burnt pink, hairs withered and frazzled, skin cracked and dry. Rawhide. His abnormally large fingers fumbled through the tiny gap to grab her arms and block her way until she could not feel the doorframe anymore. Could not hold anything.

He pushed the doors further open and stepped through into the warmth of the night.

She was staggering backwards and should be crying out; didn't know why she couldn't. Staggering backwards while he clenched her wrists together, his hands encompassed hers and wrapped her left wrist over her right. She was pinned, entangled – and she pictured chickens strung up in the market, ham hocks on chains and hooks.

She was squirming, pathetic – but not dead yet. She was not dead yet. She stamped one foot onto his, flicking her *forehead back and forth, a broken puppet, trying to headbutt him. Missing, slipping, nodding, inept, she edged further backwards until she was up against the low, tiled wall of the balcony.*

He smirked.

This was as far as she could go.

She sensed the back of her heels against the cool surface, the feeling creeping up her legs, her hips, as she pushed harder up against the short wall. This was the edge of the balcony. His face was next to hers, their arms and hands and fingers a confused tangle of limbs, over and under like a ball of wool, pushing against her chest and gullet. She could not breathe. Did not cry. But still, she leant back, her body arching over the edge, away from him, as far as she could, while he tried to wrestle her upright.

She felt the toes on her right foot touch something damp as she bowed further over, her foot slipping, sliding again, then a hand breaking free as her body jerked down violently, and they stumbled together. They staggered. They skittered.

And then she fell.

Chapter 2

You know how much I love my little flat, Susie, so you'll understand how glad I was to be back, even though Crete brought me closer to you. When I first bought it four years ago, the thought of living alone in a tight space was oppressive. I had imagined myself suffocating, withering away.

For almost twenty years, we had all lived together as a family, and then I had lived with you. Once you had moved out, it didn't seem right to stay in the house. It felt ridiculous – obscene, even. So, I considered a flat. But I feared the change.

Yet it was striking how different the reality had been. Now, I revelled in the fact I had entire control of everything – the décor, the temperature, the food I ate. No explanations, no apologies. Unlike when I had been with Tim.

Twenty-one years is a long time to be married. I was forty-four when we divorced. I thought I was old; I was wrong. It was as amicable as it could be, in its way, as we had slogged along with the marriage until the two of you were in your teens. No time is a good time for separation, but I was always thankful that you both had a settled childhood to look back on. I hope you did, at least. Not everyone has that choice, I know.

Tim and I had never been passionate, lustful, intense in our love – but we were solid and patient with one another. By the time you were older – you in secondary school, Jack in University – the four of us had started to each have our own lives, and your dad and I slowly peeled away from one another. Unstuck. Until the gap was too wide, and the bonds were lost, and it seemed to become a matter of fact that we would split before we even had time to argue about it.

So, it was just you and me in the house for a while. Until finally, I bought the flat and found myself living alone for the first time. And I loved it.

The doorbell rang.

"I hope you're not expecting haute cuisine," I said as I opened the door.

"It's nice to see you, too, Catherine," replied Jayne.

She had a bottle in one hand and peonies in the other. She lunged towards me, my friend, across the threshold in a clumsy hug. Despite my tension, I felt myself unfolding, my body recalling the safety. Her clothes had the familiar tang of fabric softener; her small, strong arms squashed me tight. She always gave whole-hearted, fully-fledged hugs.

"Of course, it's nice to see you," I replied into her shoulder. "I just got in late last night, that's all."

I was annoyed with myself for being so achy and exhausted, frustrated by the fragility of my own body. The last few years had worn away at me, down to my bones, and it was etched on my face; visible in the 20 extra pounds I was carrying; the hunch at the base of my neck, the bulge beneath my chin. But then, perhaps everyone felt that way at my age.

"I want to know everything," Jayne stated. She meant it.

Jayne and I had known each other for fifteen years. I'd been the Deputy Head responsible for appointing her as Head of Mathematics at St Ewald's. At the time, others considered it a risk – her cropped hair, severe, almost shaved back then. Heavy boots. But she was an exceptional teacher, and if you made the mistake of confusing her unconventional clothing with informality or leniency, you would come to find you were mistaken. You only needed to spend ten minutes talking to her to deduce her insight, intellect, and intent. Jayne had high expectations of everyone. At all times. Luckily, this was paired with good faith.

By the time I was Headteacher at Stockton, she was an Assistant Head Teacher herself.

"Sadly, there's not much to tell."

"Wait," she said, opening a cupboard for the glasses, "Start with the niceties. Your hotel. The sun. The food. Etcetera. Blah, blah. Go!"

I let her move around the room, finding a vase, opening the wine, and tipping a bag of crisps into a bowl for us to share. I watched her pick up the oily crumbs that fell onto the worktop and brush them off her hands into the bin. I felt an echo of previous times, a tug of affection and gratitude for her and her surprising, quiet helpfulness. She didn't look domesticated, but she threw herself into helping wherever she could. She had been a steady fixture in my flat after you died: often in the background, washing dishes, providing milk, sweeping the floor, making toast. These are the things that you need at such times. This is a true friend.

I told her about the complex where I had stayed, the strong, fresh fish I had eaten (baked in salt then set alight), and the Mythos I had drunk straight from the bottle in a tiny bar on the beach. It sounded serene. Relaxing. Like a regular holiday.

"And your tan is fab, of course," she said when there was a natural lull in the conversation. "But enough of the frivolities, now. How was it, really? Are you feeling any... closure?"

I paused. She would want to hear a yes.

"Well, I hoped to return to the taverna that Daniel had shown me last year. He said they'd gone there several times - I think most times when they didn't eat in, you know, at the hotel. I hardly took it in last year. Some bits of that trip are hazy... some etched in my memory forever, I think. This was one of the... cloudy bits. I couldn't recall the name, but I was still pretty sure I'd know it when I saw it. But I think it's gone. I couldn't find it. There was a sort of nightclub where I thought it was, a late bar, and I walked that street several days at different times, but I never found it."

"And the hotel? Hers, I mean. Susie's."

Mentally, I thanked her for saying your name. People were reluctant to do so.

"Yes," I said, "I went there... they've made some health and safety improvements and painted the place up a bit."

I heard my voice as I said 'improvements,' sour, scathing.

"God, Cath. That must be tough to see. And supremely shit that it would take something so horrendous before they thought to put measures in place."

She took a large swig of her wine with an almost imperceptible, quick shake of the head.

"I did get to meet a member of staff who remembered her, though; that was pretty much the only new information I got. Such as it was."

"Information?" Jayne asked, curiosity piqued.

Alexander had been far from keen for me to speak to his staff. He was desperate for the whole 'incident' – your tragic death – to be forgotten. Still, he acquiesced and asked me to sit on the low sofa in the lobby while he found someone. Trying to wrestle control from this irritating, unpredictable woman.

That someone turned out to be a twenty-something English waiter, known as DJ, working his second season at the hotel. DJ greeted me warmly, and had an open, easy manner about him. He asked me where I was staying, recommended a restaurant nearby, and made me promise to visit Agios Nikolaos before going home.

When I asked him about you and your death, he had less to say, and my hopes of gathering up little details – anything – started to slip away. He scratched the back of his head; I heard him breathe in through his nose.

"Yeah, I served them all a few times. At least three times. I probably wouldn't usually remember, but you know, with everything that happened... the police asked me some questions, so now it's kind of stored up in my head. Bit of a rowdy bunch but nothing major – nothing I couldn't handle. She wasn't, though, your girl…"

He spun his hand, index finger pointed, struggling to retrieve a name.

"Susie," I said.

"… Susie, yeah. Sorry." He leant in and touched my hand briefly. "She was probably the quietest of the lot."

We both sat still and silent for a moment. Picturing you, them, the evening meals.

"She was a pretty girl, eh? On the thin side, though, of course… You know, man, I really wish I could help, but I can't think of anything useful to say," he said. "The food thing was the only unusual thing I had noticed, and even then, that's not exactly much, is it?"

"What do you mean, 'the food thing'?"

He looked at me in surprise. "I did say at the time. I told them. They didn't tell you?"

"Who? Tell me what?" I asked.

"I – she wasn't eating. Hardly anything much. Well, hardly anything at all. I don't think, anyway. That's what I mean. Thin. *Really* thin."

He lifted his hands before him and held them a few inches apart. We both looked at the space between them until he dropped them down to his knees again.

"Every time I cleared their table, she had a full plate of food in front of her, sort of mashed up and mixed together. But still a full plate. It looked like she hadn't touched a thing. I remember because I

17

started teasing her about it. Joking. I didn't like it — thought she should let her hair down a bit and be more adventurous about what she ate. You know. This place isn't exactly authentic top-notch Greek cuisine, but it's alright, and it's nice to try new things, to stuff yourself silly on holiday, right?"

"Oh, but Susie wasn't fussy," I corrected him. "She'd always try anything new."

He said nothing for a moment. I could feel his scepticism.

"O.K. All I know is, she certainly wasn't eating."

Jayne sat in silence as I relayed this conversation, listening. Then as I finished, she said, "You did say how tiny she was when they brought her home."

"Yes. Yes, she was."

"So, what are you thinking?" Jayne asked, though the implication was obvious. She was being tactful, and didn't want to be the one to introduce words like 'eating disorder' or 'anorexia.'

"I don't know," I said, "It seems unlikely. She was always so strong, and confident. That's not the sort of… thing… I'd ever imagine of her… but then I never imagined any of this. I guess anything is possible."

Jayne nodded and upended the rest of the bottle into my glass.

"Next steps?" she asked.

"Well. I'll give Jack a ring. We're due a catch-up, anyway, and they were so close that if anyone knew she had a problem with food, it would be him. She told her big brother everything."

"And Daniel?" Jayne ventured, eyebrows raised.

I sighed.

"And Daniel. I'll call Daniel, too. If her brother doesn't know anything, surely her boyfriend will. Ex-boyfriend, I should say, I guess."

Though the thoughts of seeing him again made my stomach somersault.

We clinked our glasses together and then polished off the cheesecake.

Half an hour later, I was standing at my sink, rinsing glasses and plates under a hot tap. I loved this view – my tiny patio garden, with its cracked slabs and ivy, faded, mottled paintwork on the back wall. I was thinking vaguely of feeding the birds again. And I wondered why I hadn't told Jayne about the other unusual thing that had happened this week.

It had been odd. Unsettling.

When I'd arrived home yesterday, crumpled and fusty, I had found my car – my red and shiny, almost-new car – emblazoned with scratches on every door.

Chapter 3

You were not a perfect child, of course. When you were very young, up until twelve or so, you had been cautious and timid. It frustrated me how you would look to your brother, and your friends, for their opinions before expressing your own. Even with simple questions: do you need a coat? Would you like seconds? Your eyes would flit under pale, curled lashes, from your companions to the floor and back again, while you processed what you thought the consensus might be before answering.

I wanted you to be a queen, not a princess. I wanted you to be fierce, bold, and strong. And it took me several years to recognise that you were, in your own way. Just not in mine. This was my blindness – my weakness – not yours. You had a solid inner strength, but you only drew on it when you felt it was needed. When you felt it was important.

The first time you shocked me was in your first year of secondary school. I didn't make you attend the school where I worked, though I'm sure you would have accepted it if I had. I had a call to say you had a minor injury – nothing to worry about – but they needed to see me, and a trip to A and E might be in order. I raced to the school.

It transpired that a girl – Annie – had been bullying. You were holding your forearm, and it was hot, tender, and beginning to swell. Your voice sounded far away and wavering, but you didn't cry. Later we found it was broken, though we hadn't suspected it, given how little fuss you made. It took some time for me to process what your form teacher was saying.

"Sorry, no. You have misunderstood," she said as I started to rant about how it could be that they hadn't noticed you were being bullied and treated in this way – all the while feeling guilt and horror that I, too, had missed the signs. "Perhaps I'm not explaining myself clearly… Annie wasn't bullying Susie. She stepped in on behalf of a classmate – Susie was looking out for someone else."

As time went on and you grew older, you would still bow to your brother, or others, like Jessica, but not to a stranger or anyone you didn't respect. You had an impressive way of smiling, almost nodding, turning your head to one side – a gentle little bird – then stating your own opinion or preference. By the time you finished university, you knew who you were. And so did I.

The telephone rang – it would be Jack, returning my call.

"Hello, mumster," he said before I had a chance to speak. "Sorry about before. As you can see, I am very busy and important."

Jack was the manager of a Day Centre in South Wales. He had surprised everyone by working as a care worker after completing his Sports Science degree. It was a move that was supposed to be temporary, but he stayed, worked his way up, and completed various training and then management qualifications.

Now he ran a team of care staff and a catering team at a centre that had up to forty elderly clients a day. He spoke of them flippantly, but with affection. It was obvious how much he cared about them, and his job, by the fact he rarely took time off. We hadn't seen each other in four months.

"Hello, darling," I said.

I balanced my phone on my shoulder and poured water from the kettle onto a peppermint teabag, then I carried it out onto the patio and sat on my favourite, faded chair – settling into a few entertaining stories from Jack – the heat of the sun tingling my fading tan.

Forty minutes later and I was back in the kitchen, reboiling the kettle and considering whether I needed to put some woolly socks on. I had been sitting engrossed for so long, I hadn't noticed that I was sitting in the shade for half an hour. He had told me about Nicola's ridiculous accident at the supermarket ('fine, mum, she's fine!' he laughed) and about his work on their garden, and how they were hoping to rehome a rescue dog. As if he didn't have enough on his plate.

"Anyway, mum. I haven't heard much about Crete. Was it alright? Really?"

I'd been messaging him when I was away, sending photos of my apartment and the village, and several dozen of the island of Spinalonga, an abandoned

22

leper colony not far from shore, with tiny untouched beaches, faded paintwork, dilapidated stonework.

"Well, I coped. The cocktails helped."

"Or was it that barman?" He chuckled.

"The barman that was young enough to be my so– YOUR son, in fact!"

"I doubt that very much, mother. Unless the Cretans have taken to employing 16-year-old bar staff?"

I told him about the taverna being gone, as I had to Jayne, and then about what DJ had said. About the food.

Jack was silent.

"Well?" I asked.

"Surely you aren't surprised, mum," he answered.

I was taken aback. "Actually, I am."

"But she made all those excuses, on your birthday… and other times. I don't know. That barbeque thing. And that time she didn't show for Sunday lunch, you told me. You were cross with her. But I figured you were partly annoyed because she wasn't eating… Like, frustrated annoyed."

"I… I don't really know…" I said.

He paused. "You genuinely didn't notice?"

Considering Jack was rarely down south in Hampshire with us, the fact that he could recall two examples where he was present, and you hadn't eaten, filled me with alarm. And then a third when he hadn't even been there but had noticed more than me, it seemed. And remembered it all.

"Wait. Wind back. My birthday… remind me?"

Jack talked me through it step by step, and I was astounded, at how I had failed to register everything that he described at the time. But he was right. How you and Daniel colluded on your food choice and said you would swap halfway through, as you both had similar tastes. But by the time you swapped plates, you'd done little but push yours around. And then at the end, you still had a half-eaten Teriyaki Salmon in front of you.

"Remember, mum? You asked her what was wrong with it. She said something vague about it being salty or something. Remember?"

Yes, I did now – maybe – did I? And as he spoke, and talked me through the barbeque, too, I felt a series of hints and secrets come scuttling out, black, small, nasty. Like creatures under an upended rock. I could feel myself, sinking down into this new story of you.

"I can't believe it," I muttered. "It's true, I suppose. But why didn't I see?"

Jack sighed.

"Perhaps I was looking out for it. She did tell me that she and Daniel had discussed getting married, but she said she needed to lose some weight first. I remember those were her words 'needed to.' I laughed at first, as it took me aback. And she'd never been one for that kind of thing. But she was serious, as it turned out. That was the first time it struck me as a problem, as I'd already noticed she was on the thin side the previous time I'd seen her."

"They were going to get married?" I was incredulous.

"Yes. No. I – It wasn't definite. Look, I don't know. She only said it once, in passing, and I didn't pry. That's not really the point of my story, mum. And you know, you had to leave her to tell you things in her own time."

None of us had known how little time we had left to share.

"But mum, do you think this is relevant now? Does it make any difference? So what if she wasn't eating enough? How does that link to her falling?"

"I don't know… maybe if she hadn't eaten, and she was already thin… could she have had heatstroke? Been confused or dizzy?"

There was a silence.

"Jack?" I asked, unsure if he was gone, or upset, perhaps.

"She was drunk, mum," he murmured.

His voice was low and breathy, his mouth away from the mouthpiece. Pushing me away.

"I know," I answered. "Probably. But –"

"Look, no doubt she rowed with Daniel, and he didn't want to say. So what? Maybe – yeah, let's say that they argued, a bit drunk, and then she went out on the balcony. Maybe she was leaning, or looking, or doing something stupid – I don't know – but she fell. Because the wall was low. And they were in a strange place. And she was drunk."

He sounded exasperated. He had said this to me before, in numerous ways, throughout the last year, and his words were tired. He had had enough of his mother playing sleuth. He thought I wasn't accepting the truth.

"That's what they found when they investigated it," he said. "That's what Daniel said, too. So, there's no reason to think anything different, is there?"

I said nothing. Took a sip of my hot tea. I could hear some sighs and false starts down the line, as if Jack was considering, then reconsidering what he would say next. I knew my son. There was something more that he wanted to add.

"What is it?"

"You know he'd locked her out on a balcony before, do you? When they were visiting London?"

"What?"

"Her friend, what's-his-name, the musical guy. The one who produces music or whatever."

"Um… Jamie? No: Jamal?"

"Yeah. She told me that when they stayed there, they got drunk and rowed, and he locked the door behind her. He fell asleep and she was out there for hours, or something like that. I don't remember the exact details. But it was a stupid thing that went wrong. So, I've always thought that perhaps it happened again, and this time she didn't want to wait… but that still doesn't make it his fault, mum."

"Right," I snapped.

"I know what you think of him, and sure, he's never been my favourite person. But there's a huge leap between being a bit vain and annoying, to being a…"

"Yes, yes. I know that. I do," I answered.

I wasn't even sure why I didn't like Daniel. But in all honesty, I never had.

"It doesn't make him at fault. Not exactly. I mean, it makes him… It's not good if that's what happened. But we'll never know, and it's pure speculation to be throwing all of this into the mix. And… and… it wouldn't change the outcome. And anyway, she was a grown woman, mum… She should have been more careful. I mean… God, it was an accident! And she was –"

"Drunk." I finished for him.

Chapter 4

When you first met Daniel, you were captivated. Entranced. I can recall the phone call when you told me about him. You went into detail about the things he had done, achieved, and his ambitions and hopes, his attentiveness, and I felt myself walking through your description with you, stepping over clichés and absolutes. He was 'the best.' He was 'the most handsome.' The 'sharpest.' 'Sweetest.' You talked with conviction and clarity. He sounded faultless, impeccable. And to you, that was what he was, then.

He worked in Trust. He seemed successful in his job. Such a different world from yours; you were a primary school teacher. I wasn't surprised when you went into teaching – though I worried how you would cope with poor behaviour. Being brought up in a home where both parents worked in education, it seemed almost inevitable that either you or Jack would take that path, too. That is the way with teaching: teachers have teacher friends, parents, and partners. It's the sort of job that permeates your whole life. Though you surprised us all by your steely confidence in dealing with the children – going to work in some of the toughest schools in the county, and taking on Year 6, not the little ones, as I had predicted.

I was excited for you. After that first conversation, I disconnected the call and almost felt giddy, as if I were falling in love, myself. I did a little dance in the kitchen. Yet when I met him, I had to quell my disappointment to stop it from showing on my face. He was charming, of course. That was the perfect word for him. And attractive. But he seemed shallow to me. Superficial. I could not square your ardour with the man I saw before me.

That first evening we met, he spent an hour telling me about the flat he had bought at the age of twenty-one, how it turned out to be in a now up-and-coming area, and he had made a packet – but still not sold on. He was sitting on a gold mine, he said. Not in any rush to cash it in. It occurred to me that one of the reasons he liked you was that he knew you were someone who would never dig that gold, yourself.

I did not voice my concerns, transient and insubstantial as they were. I wondered if anyone would have been good enough for you. Whether I was simply old; jealous; judgemental or sour. But for some reason, I had never shaken it off, this feeling of doubt and distaste when I was around him. I did try. And I hoped you had been lucky enough to find 'the one' – after all, perhaps this was good for me, too. Perhaps now someone else could keep you safe.

But he didn't.

"Daydreaming again?" said Daniel, behind me, too close to my ear.

I jumped.

"Daniel! Hi," I replied, placing my teacup back on its saucer; I had been holding it aloft for some time. He was right.

"Well, this place is... interesting!" He smiled.

We were meeting in my favourite coffee shop. It had mismatched chairs, one wall plastered with retro and vintage posters, plants in every corner, and vegetarian and vegan food, mainly. On reflection, of course, this was not the sort of place where Daniel would usually come.

He sat down, and shuffled, trying to find an acceptable position for his arms on the table – elbows up, down, then up again. I found myself enjoying his discomfort. Then I was embarrassed by how churlish this was.

"Do you want a drink? A snack?" I asked.

He looked at the table, then to the ones on either side of ours.

"The menu's there." I pointed to the chalkboard by the counter. "The carrot cake is good."

"Sure, sounds great," he replied. "Counter service?"

I nodded.

"You want anything else?" He gestured at my cold tea.

"Just a glass of water, thanks."

I watched him walk to the counter. He was on the short side – though it didn't seem to bother him – and he was broad, muscular. He had a wide, defined jaw. Dimples. Tanned. Handsome.

Jack always said he was like a purebred Shetland pony. I smothered a grin.

When he returned, he leaned back in his chair, apparently relaxed and settled, tilting back until the wood creaked beneath his languor. He was dressed in a thin, soft jumper – a dark, salmon pink. He wore navy blue jeans, and across one shoulder he had slung a soft, brown, leather record bag, a satchel of sorts. He realised he couldn't settle himself into the position he wanted with it still strapped across him and was forced to straighten up again to remove it and hang it on the chair. After he had finished, he repositioned himself, into the same position he had been in before. I stifled a smile.

"God, sorry. I've just realised that I didn't even say 'hello'," he said, with an exaggerated cringe.

He half-stood and leaned across the table to kiss my cheek.

"I rushed here. Bit flustered… But I'm excited to see you! Thank you so much for the invite – for getting in touch again. How's retirement?"

I had been retired for almost ten months, now. After you died, I had six weeks of personal leave, then sick leave – weeks, perhaps months, and when I went back it was clear to everyone – myself included – that it was time for me to go. I had a wonderful time in my job until that point, and I'm grateful I had the support of such kind and open colleagues, who were able to talk frankly to me about the idea of moving on and support me until it happened. The school governors let me leave early – it was all very easy to resolve, in the end, as my Deputy Head was experienced and well-loved, and had been acting up competently during my absence. She stepped in.

But this all seemed like years ago, now. I didn't consider retirement a new experience to be reflected upon. This was just my way of life.

"Retirement? I'm used to it now. It didn't take long."

"No regrets, then?" he asked.

"Absolutely not."

We both smiled.

"And how's the life of an accountant working out for you?" I asked.

"Trust," he corrected, quickly. "Fine. Good, to be honest. Very good," he chuckled, knowingly.

I didn't press him for details.

"How long has it been since we've seen each other, Daniel?" I asked.

"I don't know," he paused. "I was thinking about it on the drive here. I think it must be five or six months."

We sat and talked, and as I often did, I found myself warming to him, and berating myself for my previous derision, wondering whether my judgement of him was unfounded. He had great conversational skills – a way of asking lots of questions, showing an interest, and making you feel that you were inside a bubble of intimacy with him. Yet he rebuffed compliments with flippant, self-deprecating answers and jokes. And he had open, almost flirty body language. He always sat to the side of the table, if he could, I had noticed - it felt like he wanted to jump the barrier like he wanted to be closer to you than the furniture allowed. It was flattering.

"I... Do you mind if I ask about Crete?" he asked, leaning closer still, dropping his voice.

"Well, it's only natural that you would," I said. Which didn't really answer his question.

I sighed and picked at the tablecloth.

"I'm sorry to ask, but when you said you were just back from there... well, I was eager to know how you felt. What you did."

"I went to the hotel. Alexander was there, still."

Daniel raised an eyebrow, unsure who this was, it seemed. How could he not recall such an important detail? Or perhaps it was only important to me.

"The manager. The hotel manager. It was the same guy," I clarified, "And of course, he remembered me – for all the wrong reasons – and – "

"That's an understatement," Daniel muttered.

"— Sorry?" I asked – snapped, perhaps.

"The wrong reasons, you said. That's an understatement. He'd be a monster if he didn't remember Susie's... tragedy," he said.

"Yes, of course. Anyway, there are new barriers on the balconies now. High ones. And signs everywhere. Certainly, no shortage of those. Warning signs. And they have painted the place up a bit. To be honest, it looks quite nice. You'd never think... I mean, who would ever think..." I trailed off and looked up at him over the table.

He was staring up at me from under furrowed brows, his eyes wet with tears. He made no attempt to hide it.

We both gave each other a sad smile, and then looked away.

"And did you find anything new? I am sure you'll have been hoping for some sudden, random witness or something. I know I would," he said. "I've been dying to know…" He trailed off. Shrugged his shoulders.

"Well, new for me. But apparently, I've been a bit oblivious."

"What do you mean?" he asked, perplexed.

He leant forward across the table with his hands together. For a moment I thought he was going to grab one of mine. I noted a few specks of brown sugar stuck to his right hand.

"Well, I did meet one other person. DJ, he was called. He was working there last season too, and he remembered you all."

Daniel looked away as I described him, and how he had said he had served them several times. He tilted his head, and pulled his bottom lip down, as if to indicate – yes, maybe – but also doubt, scepticism.

Again, he had forgotten a detail.

As I explained what he had told me about food, and then what Jack had said – the birthday meal, the barbeque, how slim she was, tiny – Daniel's face changed. He sat back and dropped his hands into his lap. He was frowning, now. I found it hard to read his face.

"Well, this is sort of what prompted me to contact you. I mean, it did also make me realise it had been too long, but... What do you think, Daniel? Why was she so thin? Or am I overreacting?"

He picked up a teaspoon and fiddled with it. There was a gap between my words and his that filled the space between us, the pressure increasing as it extended. A buffer, of sorts. I chose to ignore it and wait.

"She... she... had a problem with food." He was quiet. He sounded far away.

"I see," I said.

"No, I don't know if you do." There was an edge to his voice. He was obsequious, condescending. "Sorry," he corrected. "Sorry."

"Then tell me," I said.

"It was a big problem. Not just some fad or phase or quirk, or whatever. I was trying to help her. I was trying to cover for her, too, I guess. Perhaps that was a mistake..."

He rubbed his hands across his face, fiercely. I watched as he dug fingertips into his eyeballs. I felt his discomfort. He had stopped speaking but I didn't fill the void. I needed to hear more from him, and I didn't want to influence what he said or give him an easy way out.

"I was trying to help her," he repeated. "I was working with her. We talked about it a lot, you know. What food she could order that she could actually eat. I tried to talk to her about her health, then I tried a different tack. I stopped talking about weight, health, and calories altogether… I… I tried talking about wellbeing, about her future."

At the word 'future' his voice cracked and broke into a hoarse sob, though he pulled himself back together.

I nodded.

"She was ashamed. Tried to hide it; she avoided mealtimes, tried to hide her shape with her clothes. So, although she often told me she was better, or that things weren't as bad as I thought, on some level, she must have accepted the truth. She knew that she didn't look… I didn't want to expose her, I guess. That's why I didn't talk about it to anyone else, or after… You know? I wanted to protect her." He made eye contact with me, "But we talked about it. The two of us. We discussed it all the time. I just hoped no one else had noticed. Catherine, I loved her so much."

"I know you did," I said. It was true. "I can't believe I didn't spot the signs," I muttered.

"You shouldn't blame yourself," he said. "If anyone is to blame, it's…"

I shook my head. We both sat still for a moment, rooted, heavy with guilt and grief. He wiped his eyes again. I sipped my water, now tepid and flat, then cleared my throat.

"Do you think, I mean, could this have had anything to do with… With what happened to Susie?"

He leant forward and looked weary.

"No," he said. "No. I wondered that too. If there could be a connection. But I don't see how. Sorry, can I have a moment? I'll go to the loo. I just need to move, or something."

He rushed away and I started to pile up the dirty dishes on the table, automatically. I gave a wry smile: you and Jack always laughed at me and my table-clearing antics. How I brushed the crumbs onto the plate and rearranged the salt and pepper before we left any restaurant.

The server was clearing the stack of crockery when Daniel came back. He hovered by his chair, and fiddled with the strap of his bag, unsure whether to sit down. It was clear that he wanted to leave. He glanced at the clock.

"Oh," I said. "Before you go, there's one more thing I wanted to ask you. It's a bit of an odd one, so I hope you aren't going to take it the wrong way. Something that Jack said. I can't ignore it, as it seems like it could be relevant. I think he's probably got the wrong end of the stick…"

I started to tell him the anecdote about the balcony, and Jamal's flat. The locked door. As I was talking, Daniel slid back into his chair. I noticed that this time he stayed on his side of the table. No arms reaching. No sideways posture, Contained in his space. Still.

"Catherine, what exactly are you asking me?" he asked when I'd finished relaying the story. His face and voice were flat. Inscrutable.

"Well, I guess, if I'm honest, Daniel, I want to know if there was ever a time… did you lock her out of Jamal's flat? Was there ever anything that happened like that?"

37

"And did I lock her onto the balcony in Crete? Is that it?"

His words were saline, sharp.

"Yes," I stated. "Maybe."

"Jesus!" He slapped his thighs and laughed - forced a laugh. "No. I didn't lock her out onto the balcony. Think about what you're saying, Catherine. Really think about it. Really... did I lock her out?" He shook his head.

"So – what happened at Jamal's?" I persisted.

"That – yes, agreed. That happened. Sort of. But not the way you think. That was just a stupid thing. I'm surprised she even mentioned it to anyone." He paused and seemed to think for a moment.

"O.K. It was ages ago. We were visiting: a sort of budget city break. And we'd been a bit giddy, silly all day, mucking around. Every time one of us went out on the balcony, to hang washing out or drink coffee or whatever, we'd pretend to lock each other out. It was a game. In the evening we had a few beers with Jamal, and she really locked me out there for several minutes when I went out for a cheeky cigarette," I nodded, leaning into his story. "Later she went out herself, and I got her back. I locked the door. And then my phone went, and I got distracted and she must have been there for a good five, ten minutes or so... but..."

As he told the story, his eyes moved off into the distance, as if he could picture the scene. And he was smiling. He was tickled. And I could hear it, see the affection in him as he recalled it.

"The poor girl. Shit." He looked at me and snapped back into the room. "But it was ten minutes, fifteen tops. I promise. And she was tipsy, and she got herself into a bit of a state, half upset, half cross because she thought she'd have to sleep out there. Can you imagine! So no, I didn't lock her out all night at Jamal's. And I didn't lock her out in Crete," he stated.

An innocent, logical explanation then.

"That all makes sense. It really does. I'm sorry to ask, truly I am. But when Jack said that… it's just…" I didn't know how to finish my sentence.

Around me, the café was full, bustling with people and clinks. I could hear the steam of the coffee machine behind the noise of a young child asking for cake. I glanced to my left, on the table was a mound of crumbs and plates, the accidental origami of a torn and bunched-up serviette. I was disorientated, and hot.

"Look," he sighed. "The fact you would ask me that, well, I can't say it doesn't hurt. But I guess I understand," he said. "It's too much, isn't it? The not knowing. I think we've all been guilty of trying to find patterns, and answers. Reasons. You start to imagine things. But I think the truth is quite simple. She stumbled."

She tried to force the balcony door back open, but he had two hands on the handle on the other side, right elbow raised high. His arm formed a neat triangle of tension and muscle. Through the glass, she could see tightness in his face, neck turned to rope and muscle, nostrils flared, filaments of bristle on his upper lip.

A small patch of hot breath veiled the glass between them.

Again, she pulled at the door from her side. But her fingers were too small, curled, tiny, pale, delicate. Like a clutch of eggs.

She had to give up.

She jumped back, away from the door, taking two steps further onto the balcony. Her bare feet skidded on the tiles.

"Daniel, please!"

She heard the lock slide up, into position. He stepped back into the hotel room, leaving her out there. The space was dim, and his face fell into shadow. She couldn't even be sure he was looking at her from the other side.

Her heart was pounding with the thought that he might leave her there. The memory came back to her as an old wound, recalling a night coiled up on the concrete. Cold. Ashamed.

She staggered to one of the white plastic chairs and dropped down. One of the slats was splintered and she could feel a jagged scratch on the back of her leg.

The warm night air was stifling. The spaces behind her knees and in the crooks of her elbows were already damp - and her cheeks, nose, and forehead all felt sore and hot from time in the sun, earlier. Beneath her, she could hear young men, the start of an argument growing out of a joke, perhaps. Their laughter turning hot.

She tried to sit still, to collect herself, but the wine, sticky air, sunburn, shouting, scratching, and coiling, all crushed and overwhelmed her. She thought she might be sick. He was right: she was drunk.

She jumped up, unsteadily, and went to the edge of the balcony. She had not noticed before how low it was, but now as she leant over, her hands dropped down clumsily onto the wall, too far down to be comfortable. She glanced back to the sliding doors.

Daniel had pulled the sheer curtains across, but even so, through the gossamer she could see his silhouette, standing confidently with legs apart, arms loose by his side. He appeared to be watching. She could not be sure.

Seeking air, a breeze – something – she turned back towards the view. She felt her body now loose, flimsy. Her head was too heavy for her shoulders, reeling a little each time she changed position.

She lifted one hand from the wall and small green pine needles of paintwork stayed stuck to her warm palm. She brushed her hand against her shorts, but the paint fragments stayed resolutely stuck. She leant up against the wall with her full weight to steady her body and then lifted her other hand and slapped her palms together – enjoying the sudden sound that cracked the air as she did so.

Her head was hollow, peculiar. She shook it off and persisted with picking the paint from her palms.

Dark closed in from the edges of her vision and her right hand dropped to catch the balcony wall. She felt her head tumbling forwards, over the top, taking her shoulders with it. Her body jerked down, violently.

She was losing her vision, her footing, herself, collapsing in. Losing herself in space and time. Losing. Diminishing.

41

And then she fell.

Chapter 5

A basket of fruit was delivered to my house, with a note to say how great it was to catch up. There was a fresh pineapple, avocados, grapes, and an optimistic coconut that I doubted I would ever eat.

This was the kind of touch I associated with Daniel. He was always thoughtful, and generous. I remembered you telling me how he sent you a huge bunch of vibrant gerberas after your first date. In passing, you had commented on the cheeriness of them as they sat on the table on the night you met, which had been several weeks before. And he bought them for you. When challenged, he confessed later to taking a photograph of them on his phone as you went to the bathroom, saving it, showing the gentleman in the shop the blurry snap when he went to track them down.

This was the way that he was.

I texted him a thank you, and he replied an hour later to say how much he had appreciated seeing me, and he hoped we could meet again soon, as he wanted me to meet Sophie.

Sophie. He didn't explain who that was; didn't need to. The intimacy of referring to her by just a forename said everything.

This meant a shift of gear, a pulling away into the future that I was not yet ready for. I didn't want him to be ready for it, either. Regardless of my reservations about him. You had loved him.

I am a realist, and I didn't expect him to mourn you, solo, forever. But I wanted this for a while longer: because if he had a new partner, that meant he was no longer yours. And one more thing had changed.

A kaleidoscope of young, beautiful, smiling women swirled before me in my mind's eye: dark-haired, fair, petite, slender, tall, young, auburn, Asian, older, plump. None of them looked like you.

I texted Jayne and told her the news. Then I grabbed a shopping bag and went out.

Walking to the corner shop, my mind wandered back to your teenage years, before Daniel, when you and I lived alone in the house for most of the time – Jack only returning for holidays.

The divorce left you painfully quiet for a while, but in the main, you coped well. Initially, you saw Tim once or twice a week and slept over every Saturday at least. But that had waned when he moved further north. The train journey was easy, he said, when he explained to us both about the move. About an hour.

In reality, it was at least a twenty-minute drive to Southampton Central train station, and a seventy-five-minute train ride to his, if you were lucky. Most of the time there was a change involved, bringing it closer to ninety. Then there was the short walk to your dad's house at the other end, wasn't there? Strange that he never suggested a taxi. Or even went to collect you. It didn't seem to occur to him. All in all, it took up the best part of two hours each way. When it all when smoothly.

What did you think about that? Did you blame him for moving? Think you had been rejected? Or did you feel guilty, perhaps, that you didn't make the effort to take the trip more often? Because the fact remains that if you were desperate to see him – if you had really wanted to – two hours would have been nothing.

I'm not suggesting that you didn't care about each other. Of course you did. You loved each other. But it was a love built on memories, and habits. You would tease each other with the same familiar jokes. Peck each other on the cheek in the same old way. Draw on the same anecdotes, but not develop new ones. It was like a child reciting the planets, dinosaur names, and the alphabet; habitual. Easy. Cosy. Automatic. But was that all?

Our relationship was more fluid, ever evolving We grew together. Influenced each other. Ivy intertwining with trellis, gripping to bricks.

Perhaps I was being unfair. Who knows the intimacies of other people's relationships? Do we ever really know how they feel? I should not think like this. It's never attractive to be ungracious.

I was almost at the shop. It was a suburban area, and as I approached the only store for at least a square mile, I noted for the first time how I had to cross paths with other people swinging their cotton shopping bags. Buses choked the air nearby. I could feel friction as my thighs rubbed together under my skirt, and warm, damp patches beneath my breasts.

I tried to push down the hiccup of disgust that gulped up from somewhere in my belly. I had had enough of shame.

If I were to unfold, break open all my history into smaller sections, segments of my life, there were plenty of reasons why I was like this, now. No longer lean. No longer spritely, lithe. Negative. A touch bitter. And I was proud, not ashamed of most of those reasons. Proud of who I was. As I should be, I knew. I should be.

It was an unusual shop; I rather liked it. At one time it had been part of a chain, selling forlorn-looking fruit, newspapers, cheap plastic toys, and instant noodles. You and Jack had loved it – an Aladdin's cave of contraband. But I much preferred it now. It had been taken over by a young couple around eighteen months ago. They had transformed it into a cross between a bakery, a newsagent, and a market stall. They sold their own seedlings and vegetables outside the front door. They had brought in a noisy and expensive-looking coffee machine. They sold local, seeded bread. But it was still on the cheap-and-cheerful side enough to avoid accusations of pretension. Children still came here to buy cheap, fluorescent ice lollies. There was an ample canned goods section. The area wasn't upmarket enough for thoroughbred hipsters.

I was considering the cabbage and salad leaves planted up in small pots outside the shop when my phone buzzed with a text from Jayne. In reply to my message about Daniel and 'Sophie,' she said "*Ouch. I guess it had to happen sometime. Let's get breakfast or coffee next weekend. Hugs xx"*

In one sense, she was right, of course. Daniel would not stay single forever. And I had always hated judgements about the 'right' way to do things. Life is very short. We should all take any opportunity for love, laughter, friendship, and fun whenever they arise. I didn't begrudge him a future because you had lost yours. But in another sense, it struck me that it wasn't inevitable as such - *'had to happen sometime'* – because you should still be here. That was the part that was much harder to stomach.

I spent the journey back to the flat laden with an unnecessary banana loaf and visualising different incarnations of his Sophie. I marched, consciously choosing to enjoy the pulse I could feel in my face, my cheeks, and the knowledge that I had at least gained fresh air and exercise today. I was not so old and frumpy after all.

When I got back home, I was putting my key into the exterior door when I noticed something etched on the gloss paintwork. I leaned in, peering closer. Then I recoiled back again, stung.

In tiny, neat letters, right next to my doorbell, someone had tattooed the word: 'BITCH.'

***

I hadn't noticed that the light was dropping, or how much time had passed. It was only when I found myself squinting at my phone, thinking – reluctantly

47

– of seeking out my reading glasses, that it occurred to me that I was sitting in the twilight.

I leant across the dining table and flicked on the lamp.

I had been here for a couple of hours, then, picking at banana loaf and flicking through old images of you on my phone: distracting myself from the miniature graffiti at the door, perhaps. I tried not to dwell on it. I am not one to wallow or seek out extra reasons to worry.

I had dozens – hundreds, no doubt – of images of you, and yet each was familiar. Embedded in me. I found myself swiping across nonetheless, skimming stones on water, rippling, until I came across one that struck me. Then I would zoom in. Pore over the details.

Even though I had looked at them hundreds, thousands of times, it was the first time I had truly noticed how much you had changed in that last couple of years. It was a rude awakening. I must have had such a fixed picture of you, I suppose, such a complete and confident characterisation, that this was what I saw when I was with you. Not what you actually were. What I thought – no, assumed you were. We build pictures of each other, don't we? It's not always convenient to notice when the image has blurred out of focus.

There was the weight, of course, but so much more had shifted and buckled over time. In early photographs, you had your trademark scruffy, beachy, dark blonde hair; shoulder length, sometimes tied up in a messy bun or ponytail. In the last picture I had of you, it was strikingly different; cut into a sharp chin-length bob, straight and lighter. It was an expensive haircut. Grown-up.

I remember that I did comment on it, and you said it was better for work; more appropriate for your job, and easier if you ever had to work with the little ones. I accepted this readily, but I didn't replace my mental image of you with the same old saline, wavy hair you had always had. It continued to be the way I pictured you; still was, now. As if this new you were a temporary, unreal thing. It suited my image of you better, that way. It fit my worldview.

It wasn't fitting to dwell on the idea that you might be moving on, or changing, or changed. And if it ever did cross my mind that some small part of you had altered, I immediately blamed Daniel. He had made you other. He was just a phase.

Likewise, your clothes had evolved; in early pictures, you still wore what Jack had referred to as your 'hippy skirts': mid-calf or floor-length floaty, cotton clothes, paired with some sort of white blouse or vest. In my favourite picture, you were sitting at this very table, smiling at someone out of shot, almost laughing, chin up, and wearing a striking, dark red skirt. A flower from my patio was in your hair. A transient, fleeting moment had been captured – as if you were on the verge of calling out or bursting into giggles. It was a fragile thing, caught, netted forever.

I picked two images, one from your first year of teaching, and the other from two months before the accident. I saved them in a collage next to each other on my phone, fiddling around with the images until you looked the same size in them, parallel and comparable. It registered in me then, that they could have passed for two different people. Related: cousins, or even sisters. But not one and the same. They were at odds.

To the left, your smile was wide open, your skirt floor length and crumpled, your hair frizzy and wavy, fly-away, and natural. You were looking off camera again, as you were in so many images – checking on others, no doubt – and unaware. You had one arm raised, about to point, perhaps. You were not vain, and it was rare to find you posed in a picture. You let people snap away around you, without complaint but without any form of ceremony, either.

On the right, grown-up you barrelled your gaze straight down the camera, with a small pinch between the eyes and an uncertain, tentative smile. Your hair was straight and shiny, your skirt still long, but slim fitting, with a slit up one leg. You looked older, thinner, paler – poorly, perhaps.

There were two years between the images, but I wondered what had happened in that time to hasten this change. And I wondered if the change was good.

Chapter 6

It was Saturday, and I was late to meet Jayne. I was out of sorts, had lost track of time - ended up driving, and then struggled to park. I tried to avoid using petrol where I could these days, and my driving was rusty. We were meeting at a new café closer to her house than mine, and I hadn't factored in the travel time I would need, or my lack of familiarity with the area. You would have teased me, sweetheart, as I was always so fastidious about timekeeping, and always so proud of my parallel parking. Not so much these days.

The truth was, I had been avoiding using the car altogether since it had been scratched – the sheer violence involved, the pent-up anger implicit in the sharp, jagged marks made me feel uneasy. However, when I had shown the attendant at the bodywork repair centre, and asked him for a quote, he implied that he saw this sort of damage often. It was usually caused by teenagers. This had come as a relief and gave me ammunition for my theory that it was merely a random incident. So perhaps it would do me good to have used the car today, in some small way.

And now it was repainted, and you would never know the difference. No one would, as I hadn't shared the incident with anyone bar the man at the paintwork shop.

I rushed into the café to see Jayne reading a newspaper. The room was busy, humid, and smelt of baked goods and soup. It was white and modern, with industrial-style lamps hanging low over the tables from long coils of black cord. There was little to absorb the sound of the customers, or the radio that formed a backdrop behind the clatter of cutlery on plates. Against my cold cheeks and a slight headache, it felt oppressive and loud.

"Sorry, sorry, sorry!" I said as I went to sit down. "No excuse. One of those days."

"One of those days when you are a bit crap?" Smiled Jayne.

"No, I'm always a bit crap."

She laughed. "Don't worry."

She started to fold the paper away and then stopped.

"Oh, what am I doing? I wanted to show you this!"

She flipped through the paper and then opened it to a double page-spread about an art exhibition. She placed it in front of me and tapped a photograph in the top right corner.

"There: isn't that Susie's friend?"

I leaned in, to see a picture of Jessica. She looked much the same, but perhaps more drawn.

"Yes!" I cried. "How wonderful. She'll be thrilled to have an exhibition."

Jayne grinned.

"I thought it was her. I've not seen her in years, but I can still picture her and Susie giggling away in their secret club of two…. Tea?" she asked. I nodded.

Jayne went to join the small queue at the counter, and I straightened the paper in front of me, reaching into my handbag as I succumbed to my reading glasses. The exhibition featured Jessica with two other local artists, one of whom was well known, in Hampshire at least. The article was about him but did feature photographs showing four of Jessica's works. I read the short interview they had included. She said her collection was called "How It Was," and that she liked to explore different media, but this was mostly oil on canvas.

Jayne came back with a tray containing tea for two, and menus.

"We should go to it," she said.

I felt a peculiar mix of great happiness for Jessica, and to see her success, and the familiar sorrow that would so often overwhelm me - all the things you would no longer have the chance to do. Painting. Visiting galleries. Supporting your friends.

I would not cry today. Not again.

I touched Jessica's image and nodded.

"Let's eat," I said. "I'm starving."

***

It transpired that the paper was two weeks old, and that the exhibition had already been on for several weeks. There was no time that Jayne and I could find

53

to go together before it closed, which was soon. Instead, I promised her that I would contact Jessica and try to go alone. She was right, I would regret it if I didn't.

When I got home, I emailed Jessica via her website, referenced in the article. It was a simple site, but stylish and professional. I was impressed. I told her how pleased I was for her. She emailed back the same afternoon and asked me if I would like to come along one morning in the next couple of days before she took the paintings down on Thursday. The gallery would be closed, officially, but she was happy to pop along as it was close to where she lived, and she was working later shifts at the moment. I was glad to have an excuse to spend time with her. You two were so close at one stage and being with her took me a step nearer to you again, for a short while.

In my response, I passed on my mobile number, and said I'd love to go the next day if possible.

I had only seen Jessica once since the funeral when I had bumped into her at a restaurant. We had both extricated ourselves from our dinner parties towards the end of our meals and had our coffee at the bar together, standing close, taking solace in the memories that each other's mere presence gave. The bending of time and space. At that moment, we were immersed, and didn't care if we were rude to leave the people we'd accompanied out. On reflection, I'm sure they understood, anyway.

I hoped seeing her again might open up a means of making contact more frequent. An unexpected side effect of losing you was the fact I lost out on having young people in my life, too. And I missed that; I missed them. I didn't enjoy feeling old.

***

Jessica was waiting in the gallery lobby for me, fiddling with her phone. I paused for a moment before mounting the chipped stone steps, taking in her life, vigour, the vibrancy of her. She was not drawn, as I had thought. She was simply a touch older. She wore a sleeveless, fitted black dress, but had a purple chiffon scarf draped across her upper arms and back, and dark, pinkish lipstick. Her hair was loosely pinned up, and large, silver earrings hung down almost to her shoulders. She looked arresting.

She glanced up, saw me, and gave a wave.

We both moved towards the lobby door eagerly, almost skipping. I grabbed her in an enthusiastic hug, and we rocked together, swaying, and unified, for half a minute at least. There are very few people I could hold for so long.

"It's amazing to see you," she said, into my hair. "I can't believe we have left it this long."

Her voice was always edged with a slight crackle.

The door to the gallery was heavy, with a large brass knocker and layers of black, gloss paint. Jessica led the way, and took me towards the back of the building, down a tiled corridor, chattering about how lucky she had felt to get this opportunity, and that she hoped it would lead to more frequent opportunities to showcase her work. She had gained a few new contacts, one of which seemed quite hopeful, and she was determined not to let them slip away, having learnt the hard way in the past.

The exhibition was in a large, narrow room with lofty ceilings and a stunning arched window. It had an odd, sharp smell – part paint, part damp. Huge paintings were on each wall, hung with wire. In the centre of the room, a round table housed a dramatic bunch of flowers. Periwinkle was dotted amongst drooping buddleia, like dozens of tiny moths.

"Wow," I murmured.

"The light is perfect," she said. "It's a shame most people have come in the evening. You're actually lucky seeing it this way. It's the way I always picture it. The way it should be viewed."

"More than lucky. I'm blessed: perfect light, a private viewing. And I get to chat to you, too."

We walked around the room, starting with the other artists. Initially, I assumed I'd be going through the motions in viewing their work – I'd come to see Jessica's – but in fact, I was enthralled. The first artist, who I had not heard of, had painted a series of dark, almost black scenes, with red light and blue light picking out outlooks and tableaus in the centre. Up close, there was little to see, so subtle were the colourways and strokes, but from afar I saw houses alight, figures, torment. I felt transported.

The second artist's work was quite different. It mimicked graffiti, slashing and fierce, but he had juxtaposed inspirational, supportive quotes and words with the style. Neon colours against pastel thoughts. The 'inspirational' words were hackneyed clichés, though they took on a new force, made me reconsider them in these new shapes and colours. The canvases were huge, and I pictured them in a hallway – my hallway, perhaps – dominating the whole wall and greeting guests as they arrived. It was clever and stylish, but I still found more within the first pieces I had admired.

Then, finally, we came to Jessica's work. She stepped back.

"I'll leave you to view them alone for a while, and then come to chat to you afterwards. So as not to influence you!" she said. "Or to force you to be polite if you hate them."

She gave a look of mock horror, placing her hands to her cheeks in a 'scream.' Then grabbed my arm, giggling at her joke, but I could see her vulnerability. It must be an exposing thing to show others your artwork – even more so, to show people you knew. I hadn't thought of it before, although you had shared your work with me many times in the past. It must have been odd. Unmasking.

I laughed and smiled to try to reassure her.

Jessica had painted a series of triptychs, all abstract beach scenes, but strikingly varied, and inspired by different parts of the world. She loved to travel and had spent at least six months away after university hopping between countries, on a shoestring budget. I remembered that there were weeks when she had little internet access – or perhaps money, on reflection - and you had not heard from her. We used to bolster each other with anecdotes about previous times when she had been out of contact, and the exciting, outrageous things she had done on those occasions: camping in the forest; skinny dipping in waterfalls by moonlight. And then as time slipped by, I would wonder at what point I was allowed to acknowledge, out loud, that we were both worried, and perhaps there was reason to be. But she always resurfaced. Usually with a new tale to tell.

At the time, I counted myself lucky that you didn't have the same yearning to see the world on limited resources. Little did I know that danger could lurk closer to home, as well.

I stood still to take in the paintings and their intense, sparse beauty. Often, there were bleached sections, white hot, crashing severely against blue, black, or indigo thunderous skies. Some of them looked familiar, perhaps from further down the coast nearby: Devon or Cornwall, I thought.

I pulled over one of the stools that were pushed under the central table and sat two metres away from her final piece, which I knew to be Crete.

"Did you spot me?" she called out, as she crossed the room, coming back towards me.

I was bemused. "No. Where?"

I looked around the room then, wondering if she had been a model and I had missed her.

"Here."

She pointed out that hidden within an outer panel in each series she had painted herself into the scene – tiny, almost imperceptible, but the same green dress marking her out each time. I stood up and went to the picture of Crete. In it, her head was dipped, and one hand was on her face. I reached out and wanted to touch it.

She came closer to me and placed a hand on my shoulder.

"God, I miss her," she said.

We talked about every triptych in turn, where the beach was located, what it meant to her, and why she had chosen to paint it. We talked about the names she had given to each piece, who had bought her work, how they had taken weeks to complete – so in fact, her hourly rate was abysmal.

"Susie sometimes said she'd regretted not going to Art College," she said, straightening a nameplate.

"Did she?" I hadn't ever heard you say so.

"Her drawings were extraordinary. I was never able to sketch the way she did. So precise, detailed. She was so patient."

It was true.

"I wish I had some of her work," I said. "She took her portfolio with her when she moved out. But I do have a Mother's Day card she made me a few years back…"

I wondered where it was. Made a mental note to dig it out when I got home. It struck me how private you had become over your art, as time went on. I hadn't seen your work for years. Perhaps the idea of an exhibition was ludicrous, even had you lived. I hoped not. I may be biased, but you did have extraordinary talent. I encouraged you to continue with your art. Life is short, and gifts such as this should be cherished and watered and appreciated. I had wanted you to continue with it, and to share it.

But perhaps I had not impressed this on you enough, I considered. Perhaps I should have said more.

We both seemed to feel it was time to move away. Jessica took me into a small kitchen, hidden down a corridor housing cleaning equipment, and coat stands. We continued to chat with the ease that comes from having known someone for so long, and the unspoken, unbreakable connection that comes from shared grief. We would always be linked.

Apologetically, she made me an instant coffee with long-life milk and poured herself a glass of tap water: such a sharp, ironic contrast to the expensive, high culture of the artwork. I didn't care – hadn't dared decline the offer for fear of cutting our meeting short.

After a while, I told her about meeting up with Daniel, even telling her the story of my asking him whether she'd been locked out that night. I cringed as I relayed it. The implicit accusation sounded even worse as an anecdote.

"Honestly, I don't really know what I was thinking," I said, shaking my head. "I'm embarrassed now. Accusing him of trapping her out there. Basically, saying it was his fault…" I faltered. "What a bitch."

"No," she stated. "It was a perfectly understandable question."

"Do you think so?" I asked.

"Daniel is no saint."

There. There it was. But I often found myself unsure whether things had the significance I attributed them with when it came to you. Jessica's words could mean anything from the fact he left his pants on the floor, to being some sort of criminal mastermind. I could feel the old confusion rising in me again, the questions flickering, blooming open. I couldn't bear this uncertainty, this unease. I wanted to shut it all down. I didn't know what to ask to quell this feeling. But it was there; still there. The disbelief. The questions.

"She was drunk," I said, perhaps to myself. "She fell. I don't know if any other details really make much difference. She'd still be gone."

"She wasn't that drunk," she said.

I sipped at the bitter coffee. It was both too strong, and yet too milky at the same time.

"Let's go outside," Jessica said, after a beat. "I suddenly feel claustrophobic here."

We walked back through the exhibition, and she pushed open the fire door, which led out onto a pretty, but tatty, garden. The heavily scented air of the gallery was pierced open by the noise and breeze. Well-established bushes grew around the edges of a patio, broken slabs bulging and sinking and cratered with dandelions. I felt a sudden relief to be back outside.

Jessica took out a pack of cigarettes from her handbag.

"The night she died," she said, quietly. "She had hardly spoken two words all evening. I hadn't seen her much that day as I'd stayed at the hotel, but she and Daniel had gone off to the beach together. She had a pink nose and strap marks by the time they

61

returned. Somehow, he was tanned and lovely, as usual."

She smirked and rolled her eyes.

"We all met for dinner, and I wanted to sit with her, to chat, you know? It was, what, four days into the holiday? Sorry, I should know. I try not to think about it too often these days. I find it... counterproductive. Anyway, somehow, I had hardly seen her at all. For four whole bloody days. But he channelled her down to the end of the table and sat next to her. He had this way of sort of holding his hand mid-air, palm flat, directing, guiding her into her seat. Like some sort of bloody traffic conductor. I didn't know if it was romantic or domineering," she paused. "I still don't."

She acted the movement out, and I pictured him as she did so. It was a familiar gesture.

Jessica took a deep drag.

"She was wearing a short dress, above her knee. I remember it struck me that she didn't usually show her legs. Those skinny little legs."

I hesitated, then broke in.

"She changed the way she dressed in the last year or two, didn't she? Don't you think?"

Jessica nodded but didn't look at me. She seemed far away, and I could feel myself losing my footing, untethered. I wanted to halt it. I gazed back through the window to the buddleia, the periwinkle, the beaches.

"I didn't get to talk to her that night," Jessica stated, "I've always regretted that."

Chapter 7

I was absorbed in a radio drama, about to start chopping vegetables for dinner, when my mobile phone rang. I looked at the screen: Daniel.

"Hello?"

"Hi! Catherine, sorry, look... I know this is last minute, but we are going to be around the corner from yours in five minutes or so. Sorry. Look, I guess it's cheeky, but I was wondering if you were in. Could we stick our heads in? Me and Soph, I mean, five min, that's all."

I could hear the smile in his voice – pictured him looking at Sophie as he spoke to me, holding her hand or reaching up to touch her cheek.

"Um." My mind went blank. I had no reason to decline. "Sure, O.K." I winced at my flat voice, unwelcoming tone. "I mean, yes, of course! Great."

"Great," he repeated. "See you in five."

The phone went dead. I was still holding the knife. I dropped it onto the chopping board and moved everything onto the side next to the sink, half-heartedly covering it with a tea towel and wiping down the surfaces. I piled up the junk on the dining table into one mound, instead of the obstacle course of newspapers and bills that I usually navigated at dinner time. I turned on the lamps and changed the radio station to music, then sprayed the room with a floral scent to hide the sharpness of the freshly cut onions. That would have to do.

I felt exposed at the idea of him being here. Vulnerable.

Would you have wanted me to let them in? I suspect that you would.

I took a bottle of wine from the fridge and poured myself a large glass. By the time the bell rang, ten or twelve minutes later, I had almost finished it.

Sophie was short, slim, and dark-haired. Nothing like any of my imaginings. She was younger than you, which surprised me as Daniel must have been twenty-nine by now. I guessed that she was twenty-five, at most. Twenty-three, even. She smiled at me, nervously, and crunched her eyebrows together in the middle – and I was glad that she at least had the sense to recognise this was odd, uncomfortable.

Daniel did not: or at least he didn't acknowledge it, if so. But then Daniel was friendly, gregarious by nature. Or self-absorbed? I shook the thought away.

They followed me in, holding hands. I noticed Sophie pull hers away and step onto the other side of me as we came into the kitchen area.

"So, are you two off out somewhere nice?" I asked, collecting two glasses, and starting to pour.

"Arts' Centre. Supper and a play," he answered.

I should have asked what they were going to see, but I didn't think I could bear to hear it.

"I didn't know you liked the theatre," I commented.

Daniel shrugged, and gestured to Sophie, vaguely. "No wine for me, please."

Sophie had put her hand over one of the glasses.

"He's not making you drive, is he?" I joked.

She smiled. "Yes and no. Could I have water? I'm happy with that."

"I have soda if you want to water the wine down?"

"No, honestly. Water is fine. I don't really drink," she said.

"She's not like—" he paused. "She's not like us." Daniel said with a smile. "She's a good girl, aren't you, Soph?"

I resented the implication; felt a shudder of irritation but tried to remind myself not to be sensitive. He had meant nothing much by it. Don't judge. Don't be snippy. He's making small talk. It's only a joke.

We chatted about Sophie's job (she was the manager of a large clothes shop); Daniel told me how his brother was moving to America, and his mum recently retired; I told him about Jessica's art exhibition. His eyes lit up.

"Jess!" He shook his head, "I haven't seen her in…well, I can't think, actually."

"I like art – we could go? It might be fun," said Sophie.

"You're a right little culture vulture, aren't you?" He teased.

But I explained how they were too late. The exhibition hadn't run for long, and it was now over. A small, unpleasant part of me was glad he wouldn't get to see it, I admit. I wanted to keep the pictures, the experience – Jessica – for myself. And Sophie,

65

nice as she was, should not be viewing paintings of the place where you had died. This would be wrong, in dozens of inexplicable ways.

"I've got a flyer though," I said. "It's got some of her work in. I'll get it: hang on. Then you can get an idea of what it's like."

I went to the bedroom to look for my handbag, where Jessica had stuffed a handful of leaflets as I left. I was only gone a couple of minutes but when I came back, they were kissing. Daniel had come around to where Sophie was, with his back to me. He was standing with his feet apart, both hands on her face. She had her hands by her side. I wondered how passion could spark in such a short time – in moments. I wondered why it would flare here. I stood still at the edge of the doorway into the kitchen, not knowing whether to disturb them and not wanting them to know that I had seen. Had he kissed you the same way when people left the room? A sphere of intimacy, caught for a few seconds when crowds dispersed. A cesura.

Sophie saw me first and broke away.

"Here we are," I said, striding in and not acknowledging the kiss. "You can keep it. I have several."

Daniel smiled his thanks, unabashed, and folded the flyer into his pocket without looking at it. He downed the end of his drink.

"We should go, Soph… Thanks so much for inviting us in. I really wanted you two to meet." He was earnest and made hard eye contact with me. Again, I found myself feeling guilty, and lost.

66

They followed me to the front door, but Sophie stopped in the hallway, to look at the pictures of you on the radiator shelf.

"Ah! This is Susie," she stated. "I'd recognise her anywhere. What wonderful pictures."

"Really?" I asked, taken aback that she had seen you before, and that she took the time to stop and look again, now.

"She is photogenic, isn't she? I wish I looked like that in pictures."

She cradled a picture frame in both hands, carefully, and then replaced it. She looked up at me.

"You must have happy memories."

I nodded, touched by her words. Few people take the time to use your name, ask about you, or talk about the time when you were alive. Most of them focus on your absence, now, instead. Death does that. It robs life – the past as well as the future. I couldn't help but like this girl, with her simple sincerity; though, of course, I didn't want to.

"I've seen Daniel's pictures from Christmas, and on holiday. She's smiling in every single one. Or laughing, maybe. Very natural. You can tell she was a good person. Nice to be around."

"She liked a social gathering," said Daniel, vaguely, undoing the latch of the door.

He kissed my cheek and stepped over the threshold, then she followed him out, taking care to straighten the photo she had last admired.

"Thank you," I said, patting her shoulder. I wasn't sure exactly what I was thanking her for.

"It was lovely to meet you," she said, as I closed the door.

But as I stood in the hallway after they had left, his words rankled, tarnishing hers. You weren't a social animal. You didn't enjoy gatherings or partying, or any of those things. It wasn't true. You liked to see people happy, and to put people at ease, yes. But I hated that your ending seemed to have distorted your story. You always made an effort. You were everyone's girl, but not outgoing, or gregarious. You were everyone's solid, quiet friend: even hers, now. Sophie's. Sweet as she was, even she had a piece of you.

She tried to shut the door, but she fumbled. He was up close, brushing skin to skin. Hot. Distracting. She was reaching over his shoulder to push the door behind him. The filaments of bristle on his upper lip brushed across her neck.

Finally, the door clicked shut. She leapt away, taking two steps into the hotel room as she turned, twisting in a fractured pirouette. Giggling, light.

Her feet skidded on the tiles as she raced towards the balcony. She could hear him following behind, eager, desperate. She kicked off her sandals, and then yanked the sliding doors open, enough to squeeze through.

She was almost on the other side, one hand still on the handle, and he was there. His hands were there. A forearm tanned, hairs sun-bleached and frazzled, skin glowing with the sun, and hunger. Beautiful. Warm. Large fingers, imposingly large, were searching to grasp her arms, her torso, her clothes, to block her way - until she could not feel the doorframe anymore. She could not feel the evening breeze. She could not feel anything but this.

She was staggering backwards. Staggering, as they locked together in one; her tongue seeking his, his hands pulling at her clothes, pressing at her skin. He stood with his legs taut, apart. And she was transported in the air; pictured dandelion clocks ready to explode in the wind.

They edged further until she was up against the low, tiled wall of the balcony.

He pulled away from her face, smirked.

She felt the back of her heels against the cool surface, the feeling creeping up her legs, her hips, as she pushed further against the short wall. She was propped on the edge of the balcony. His face was next to hers, their arms and hands and fingers a confused tangle of limbs, over and under like a ball of wool, pushing in a mass against their torsos. She could not breathe. She leant back, her body arching steeply over the edge, as he lifted her skirt. She drew a sharp breath.

He yanked one arm away from her and pulled at his flies, trying to rip apart buttons from their holes, rushing, frantic.

But she sensed the toes on her right foot touch something damp; her foot slipping, sliding, then her right-hand buckling beneath her as her body jerked down violently, and she tumbled.

She saw his face – a flickering film reel of lust blinking into confusion, flashing into panic.

They both lifted their hands, seeking hands, fingers lacing the air, missing, inept, never touching. Never quite reaching one another.

And then she fell.

Chapter 8

Jessica texted and asked if I was free to meet. I invited her to the flat for coffee – no one had been in it except me since Daniel and Sophie came. I felt I could still sense him, smell him here. Sour. Irritating. And Jessica is always a fresh breeze. Well, you know what she's like. It was just what I needed.

You always loved old films, and when Jessica joined the school for Sixth Form you were intrigued by her from the moment you saw her Marilyn Monroe t-shirt. While the other students were listening to Taylor Swift and playing Farmville, you two would sit in our living room under a duvet and watch Doris Day sing about the Deadwood Stage. It was a sharp contrast to your ultra-modern values or her pierced nose, and yet somehow it worked.

Within six months you had blended and meshed your relative styles and quirks, hanging off each other's arms and words in a medley of vintage clothes and home-dyed hair.

I am sure that you must have argued at some stage, but I don't recall it now. The shards of your relationship that flick in front of me whenever I think of the two of you are ephemeral, and they are nothing but giggles, sketchbooks, and support. Perhaps this is the unreliable memory that a mother's grief holds, simply to make things more bearable. Or perhaps it is the truth. Either way, I am grateful to be able to think of happy times, a vivacious you, an untainted you, sometimes.

I used to feel guilty if I ever thought about good times. As if I was diminishing the horror of your passing, somehow. Somehow, I was expected to let that dreadfulness topple over and swallow everything else. I know you would say that was silly, my darling girl. But I felt as if I was shallow, too quick to move on, or in denial. But now I know that these memories are as real as the bad ones, equally, if not more important. And it is not possible to sustain the stress and pain of sorrow every minute. Or I would die from my grief.

I'd like to pretend I made cupcakes or a sponge when she came, but I went to the shop and bought another banana loaf. I was glad to have reason to stretch my legs. I had started to think that they got them in just for me.

She arrived promptly, and after some chatter about the weather and her walk from the bus stop, we went outside. We sat on the patio with a cafetière and chatted about her plans. She was working part-time for a women's charity: the paintings didn't pay the bills. The charity didn't pay well, either, but that was understandable. Yet between the two things she had enough to get by. It was erratic and insecure, but so far, she kept her head above water, and there were odd moments of unexpected wealth when she would buy herself new clothes, a bicycle, and a phone.

She was renting a room in a shared house, she said shyly, but a nice enough one: they had a large, communal kitchen where they often ate together, and she even had an en-suite. The low rent allowed her to keep a financial buffer, needed for her line of work. She laughed at the term 'savings' and said it would be overstating things to call her bank balance such. But she was safe. I could tell there was a part of her that was ashamed of this lifestyle or thought I would judge her. I didn't: in fact, I felt a twinge of envy. There was a social, wholesome, unpretentiousness to it. I felt middle class and stagnant in comparison. She shuddered when I asked if she had any longer-term plans.

I changed tack and told her then about Daniel and Sophie coming around.

"He did what?" she asked, incredulous, sitting up and twisting around towards me. "Jesus. How did that make you feel?"

"Well, off balance, I guess. It was…odd."

"I'll say. What an insensitive bastard."

I laughed.

"No, I mean it!" she said, riled. "What on earth was he trying to achieve? Why would you want to meet his new missus?"

I shrugged. "She seemed lovely. A very thoughtful girl. And I rather think he wanted my blessing, somehow."

"That's a much more generous interpretation than what's going through my mind."

"Oh, and what is that?" I asked, but she shook her head and looked away.

"I thought you liked him?" I asked, after a brief pause.

"I don't – I don't exactly dislike him. To be honest, I don't really trust him. And I was never sure he was right for Susie, that's all."

I considered this. Her words from the gallery came back to me, resurfacing: Daniel is no angel.

"You don't trust him?"

"I mean, I'm not suggesting something untoward with Susie's fall, you know. I don't think he's evil or anything, but…" she trailed off.

"So, was he disloyal? A womaniser, I mean?"

"A cheat? No, not at all." She chuckled, sardonically. "I doubt that very much. He's too proud of himself for that. Likes to take the moral high ground. No, that's not the sort of thing I mean, either. There's just something about Daniel that's so bloody fake. Disingenuous. And self-absorbed. I always thought that everything he did was for his own benefit somehow. Not hers. Or for show. But I guess that doesn't make it all his fault. Right? Even fake twats can go through awful experiences that aren't of their making, I guess."

Trust is a funny thing. We use the word as if to make a judgement on the other person sometimes, as if it must mean that they are not trustworthy if we don't have faith in them. It must be their fault. And, of course, I could relate, because I had experienced those moments of doubting him, too. But neither of us had any concrete reason not to, as far as I could see. So perhaps the problem was with us, after all. It wasn't that he wasn't untrustworthy. It was that we had a lack of trust.

"You know I always wondered if someone else was there," I muttered.

I hadn't voiced this thought in so long, as others – Jack, Tim, for example – were irritated when I did. I hadn't meant to say it then, either. But Jessica nodded.

"It was all very odd. I get it. I understand why you'd think that. I still can't imagine how it happened," she said. "I can't picture it. Not that I want to. But for a while it was all I could do to stop myself from running through scenarios, you know?" I nodded. "I don't, now. I don't let myself. But I'd like to know it was a simple trip, that's all."

"Drunk," I said, breathlessly, "But then, the other day, you said she wasn't that drunk? And her bloodwork wasn't so bad – the tests they did on her blood, I mean. People keep telling me that's it, that's the reason, but I never thought of her as a party girl or a big drinker. And certainly not a reckless one."

"She wasn't," said Jessica. "Please don't think of her that way."

"It's like people are redrafting her to fit into their storyline. Like it's simpler that way. Like then it could make sense. But she wasn't. She wasn't like that,"

I was threading the words in the air, collecting them like scattered beads and bringing them together, one by one. Into a chain. Out loud.

"I know."

I leaned over and squeezed her knee.

"Thank you," I said.

We sat for a moment, drinking our coffee. The autumn light was soft; the sun warm, but a breeze tinkled in the background, buffering my flowers, and taking leaves off my shrubs, depositing them onto the patio, periodically.

"The reason I came was to give you something, actually," she said, placing her cup down.

She passed me a cardboard tube that had been poking out of the top of a hessian shopping bag. She looked timid, younger for a moment. I leaned over and took the end of the tube and levered it open. Inside, there were prints of the Crete scene from the exhibition – giclée paper, a limited run, I could see from the numbers scratched into the corner. I was overwhelmed.

"I'm just sorry I couldn't give you the real thing. I don't know if you noticed, someone had bought it. I don't know who – it was direct with the gallery. And I know it was my work, but I'm not sure that I could have afforded to be that generous anyway. I mean, that's at least a month's rent for me but I'd still only be making minimum wage if you added the hours up… God, that sounds awful. It's all immaterial anyway. Sold."

She wasn't so much addressing this to me, as voicing an old grudge, and an unnecessary explanation. People often overlooked the amount of time – and resources – that went into each work. And she'd had plenty of friends and family expecting freebies and favours in her time, as well. Somehow, many people who were close to her thought it distasteful for her to charge them full price, and she had been on the receiving end of plenty of requests for murals, and wedding card designs, leaving gifts, Valentines' presents, sketches in her time. If she had done them all – and she did do many – there would have been no time left at all for her paid work. There had even been an occasion when a distant cousin had asked for a painting commission and had assumed that he would get it for free. An argument ensued. Jessica had come to our house in tears.

I thought back to you, painting at the table. How long it took you, even as an amateur, all those years ago. For Jessica, there would be twice the work and ten times the pressure.

"…But I could see you liked it, so I thought you might appreciate this."

"Thank you so much," I said. "You were such a good friend to Susie and me. You still are. You're a good friend."

But she looked away and tilted her head, and an almost imperceptible twist of her lips showed me that she didn't agree.

***

University was an easier transition for you than I had expected: easier than secondary school had been, at least. The confidence you started to gain from your friendship with Jessica helped no doubt, and the eclectic mix of people you came across once you got there. Until then, although you had always had friends, Jessica was the only one that you had a true synergy with. University proved to you that the world is made up of a spectrum of people. Your life in Hampshire had only shown you a handful of the colours of the rainbow, so far.

You came back that first Christmas with the same hair, the same skirts, but a renewed vigour. This was the incidental potency of finding your tribe. You talked more than I had ever known you to, about your new friends, your new social life, studies – though not about boys. You had little time for them, back then. You spent that first evening home eating my lasagne with salad at the table, illuminated by the candle you had bought me from the University shop, revelling in the fact that Jack was snorting at your anecdotes, for once, rather than the other way around.

I remember my pride, wedging my mouth into a smile that lasted so long my jaw began to ache. And then I remember that selfish pang, that doubt, as I stood over the kettle in the kitchen and it struck me perhaps you had shifted away from home for good, and whether you would ever come back permanently, and also whether you and Jessica would be as you had been. I loved seeing you two together, and it hadn't been all that long since you had established that partnership, of sorts.

My worry was unfounded and brief. After uni, you came back to the area and always lived within a short drive of my house. And it was only the second day, that first Christmas when I came back from the supermarket to find you and Jessica together on the sofa. You were a butterfly print of each other, turned ninety degrees to face one another, long skirts overlapping, crumpled, and bracelets and slender arms tied into accidental knots. And it remained the same, each time you saw each other, no matter how long you had been apart.

So, I refused to believe she had ever been anything but a great friend to you.

The next evening, I had a text from Jessica.

Bumped into Sebastien and told him I'd seen you. He asked if he could have your number. I said I'd best check.

Sebastien. I had only met Sebastien twice, as far as I could remember. At your 25th birthday, for one. Of course, I would recognise him, knew a few vague stories of his exploits and he was one of the people who had been with you in Crete. One of the first on the scene. He was a nice enough young man, from what I had heard, and you two had been good friends at one stage – but my memories of him were hazy. I was surprised. What could he want?

Part of me was excited at the thought, in spite of its peculiarity. Another step closer to you. Another excuse to walk through stories and memories again. I finished my cup of tea and then texted back: *Of course x*

She replied instantly. *Great! I know he'd like to see you too xx*

So – he didn't just want to speak, or text, he was hoping to meet up. The words dangled in front of me in a tease; I hoped he wouldn't wait too long to get in touch.

By the time I woke the following morning, he had already texted me and asked me how soon we could meet.

But the same day, Nanna died.

Chapter 9

One of my regrets is that you did not get to know your Nanna better. Granny – my mum –died when you were so young that I am sure you didn't remember her. She was a fierce, bold woman and I have her in my veins. She lives on for sure, and my thoughts of her are rarely sad, but founded in humour. It is a warm blanket to think of her, in her sequined, sparkling tops, familiar, comforting. Quite different than to think of the loss of you. It was an expected loss, and she was prepared, as was I. Quite different.

Nanna – Tim's mum – was much more like you. She was a consistent, measured, reliable person and I admired the purity of her values and character. She was little and calm, but she knew exactly who she was. She had a way of resolving an argument. Her words fell, landed home, rather: her integrity settling as soft and silent snow. I was often speechless after she had gently corrected me or Tim.

She was a better person than me.

When Tim called me, mid-morning, something had to be wrong, and for a moment I panicked that it was Jack. Silly, really. Nanna – Rose – was 91 and had been ill for at least two years. I should have thought of her. I can be quite self-absorbed, sometimes. Believe me, sweetheart, I'm not proud of it.

Tim asked if I wanted to come to the funeral and I didn't hesitate. Jack was going, he said, though I would have gone either way. He had just spoken to him, and Jack was already researching to sort a hotel for us both. I breathed a sigh of relief, having been worried that Tim might suggest I stay with him. Watching him reuse the same coffee mug for 24 hrs, or draining overcooked vegetables haphazardly using the saucepan lid, would rankle after attending a funeral.

I know that's petty. I do know it.

All of this meant that I had to text Sebastien to cancel the plans we had made for that weekend, as I would be taking the train the same day, ready for a funeral on the Monday.

***

Jack knocked on my hotel door just before seven, ready to walk me down to the hotel bar to meet Tim. A tangle of thoughts and emotions entwined within me – ridiculous, given how long we had been divorced. I would have much preferred to have gone to a Balti House with Jack than a fish restaurant with Tim, but at the same time, this was sullen of me. Rose had not long died. And it would be good to talk and think of her.

You know how often your dad is late, so we had planned a swift drink alone before he arrived. Even Jack liked a bit of liquid courage before seeing him,

I think. We were stood in the bar, packed with businesspeople with loosened ties and half-drunk pints of Guinness and lager. It was the type of hotel that had pretensions to be smarter than it actually was, with an ornate, stained glass feature semi-circling above the bar, and modern chandeliers hanging low, on long chains, over tables. The place even had a signature scent – the same oils infused the soap, the reed diffusers, and now the candles. Bergamot and allspice. All this, in spite of the fact that my room was box-sized and simple, a hard bed with thin sheets and not enough pillows. You know the sort of thing I mean. I was halfway through my drink, a large gin and tonic, when Jack tapped my inner elbow subtly, and I knew he was approaching from behind me.

He still had that crumpled linen jacket, pale green, darker at the cuffs – either wear and tear or dirt. That same jacket. Can you believe it? His haircut hadn't changed, though a little longer, lighter, and otherwise he looked much the same, but with jowls and a paunch. He might well have said the same of me.

He leant into one cheek and kissed me with his hard, dry lips. Then he grabbed Jack's hand and pummelled it up and down, and for a beat too long. I thought Jack looked as if he was about to hug him, stepping forward with arms wide, and adjusting just in time for the handshake.

"I'm so glad you both came," he said. "Thank you."

He stood with both his arms raised, almost encircling us, almost touching us, but not, and it struck me that this was true.

"Let me get you a drink." I didn't ask what he wanted; it was always the same thing.

We moved to a table once his Chianti had arrived, and Jack managed to fill the void of awkwardness by rattling away lots of stories I had already heard, about his garden; his colleague; the new gym he attended. Tim said little, except to ask a few gentle questions, and it made me nervous. It was often hard to know what he was thinking, even when we were married, so I was glad to let Jack do the work. I found myself smiling into my drink, picking at the skin next to my thumbnail with my index finger until the quick began to bleed. I looked down and found my skirt freckled with tiny red splatters, my thumb worm-skinned, deep pink, etched with cracks. Foolish.

After about half an hour we relocated to the restaurant, which was only five minutes away. As we walked down the street, I listened as Tim opined about the veal, and blushed when he chuckled that I tripped slightly (twice) on irregular slabs in the pavement. This was not like home.

It was a disarmingly modern establishment. Shiny. I could never understand how Tim could be such a snob about his food, so up-to-date, stylish - and yet dress poorly and behind the times. But then, we all value different things, I suppose.

"What about you, dad?" Jack asked, once the menus arrived. "What have you been up to?"

"The usual, I guess… Oh! but I did have a rather fun stint teaching supply at a boys' school. I did a full three weeks. First time in a few years."

"Supply?" I asked. "I didn't think you did that anymore. I don't think I could face it."

"Neither did I. But actually, I enjoyed it. I might carry on. It keeps you young." He raised both eyebrows and looked back to his menu, then gave a smile that was almost giggling. I wasn't sure if it was a dig at me and my ageing girth. Or maybe he was trying to say he'd met another young Teaching Assistant or Art Teacher. It wouldn't be the first time, though I hoped the days of wooing student teachers were behind him.

"Did it pay well?" asked Jack.

"Enough for a long weekend in Europe, I guess."

This was an oddly specific analogy.

"Mum's not that long back from Crete, aren't you mum?" I gave him a glare – I didn't want Tim encroaching on that part of my life.

"That was a few weeks ago now," I said.

"Right… I was thinking of going to Malaga. Susie used to go on about it. Told me a couple of great stories."

I flinched at the mention of your name.

"Susie?"

The waiter came for our order and the moment shifted along. Tim tried to take command of the ordering process, and for a moment it seemed that we would all be having the veal, in spite of my objections - but the waiter stood by, quietly, with a faint smile, and then turned to me and simply said: "Madam?".

I ordered a seafood massaman curry.

Tim went to the bathroom after our order was taken, and I enjoyed the respite. The air came back into the room, for a moment. I caught the scent of olive oil and lamb as a waiter strode by and was transported back to Crete. Lemons. Courgettes. Hollow, desperate sadness. I sometimes thought I might visit, again, as if I should, somehow. Perhaps I would.

Then I recalled what he had said.

"Jack, dad said something about Susie, then... Malaga? But it's not that long ago she went there, just a few months before, I mean... you know. So, were they communicating, then? Friendly, I mean?"

"Yeah," he looked awkward, "They spoke a bit more in the last few months before... towards the end. They were kind of back in proper touch again."

I had no idea. I couldn't process this information. Couldn't make sense of it. It didn't fit.

Tim returned around the same time as the starters, and our conversation moved back to food and drink, and décor. After a while, Tim began yattering about Rose's flat, the wallpaper in her bedroom which had been the same for twenty years, how she had her living room decorated and then bought an identical Axminster carpet. I had heard these tales before, and they were vaguely amusing, but it would be a comfort to him to talk about her, and this gave him a sort of excuse. And it made the evening comfortable.

"Wow, I remember her kitchen," Jack said. "You could probably sell it for a ton now... Vintage!" He laughed, affectionately.

"If the cupboard doors didn't spin like a frisbee every time you tried to open them." Tim smiled.

They chinked their glasses together.

We all paused for a while, eating, or pushing food around our plate as we considered Rose, and the fragility of life. The way children are anchored by their mothers. And how we are all children to our mothers.

We were almost finished with our meal when I felt able to ask what had been on my mind for the last hour.

"You said you might go to Malaga? Something about Susie?" I tried to sound casual, as I gathered up my side plate, and breadcrumbs and stacked them as neatly as I could with my cutlery on my dish.

He tilted his head.

"Yes, she loved it there, didn't she?"

"I... well, I know she went. But I didn't realise you guys had chatted about it. Did you catch up much in the last couple of years? You... you never said."

"In the year before she died in the accident, you mean."

He said it kindly, prompting me out of my old habit of denying your absence. Not saying the words.

"Yes, that's what I meant."

He told me how you had started to establish regular Monday evening chats. Not every week, but often. How you had talked about friends, asked for

87

his advice about teaching, compared notes on holiday destinations.

"Why didn't you say?" I asked.

Tim chuckled.

"I wasn't exactly withholding it, Catherine. It's not like you and I sit down and have cosy chats very often. Can you honestly say you tell me everything? Or even many things? Anything?" He said it with affection.

I considered this.

"Well, no, of course not." I paused. "Fair enough," I conceded.

"So, we've never really had the chance, have we? To talk about those sorts of things. It was pretty… chaotic around the time of her death and my weekly catch-ups with her didn't seem the most pressing fact."

I supposed this was true. All our conversations were about travel insurance and the police and repatriating you. And I was the one who avoided talking about anything too personal. Too human. Not Tim.

But what made less sense was the fact that you had not mentioned it to me, either.

The waiter came and topped up our glasses, and took away the plates I had stacked so neatly, as I always did. We ordered coffee: him a double espresso and an Irish whisky chaser, me a macchiato.

"Macchiato," he repeated quietly, amused, into his lap. I tried my best to ignore this.

"And what about Daniel?" I asked. "Did she say much about him?"

"A little." He shut the question down.

"Tim," I faltered. "I... looked back at some pictures. I don't really... I can't explain it, but I hadn't noticed quite how thin she was. Jack knows." I glanced at him, but he was gazing at the table. "Did she...? Did you ever talk to her about food? And –"

"No," he said. He sighed.

"– do you think she was happy? O.K.?"

I could feel the tears pricking, again. Not again.

"No," he said, again.

"No, you didn't talk? Or no, you don't think she was happy?"

"Both. I did talk to her. But not about food. Or much about her mood. I gather that was Jack's department..." He looked proudly toward his son. "But she didn't seem very happy. I mean, she wasn't open with me. Not really. But she gave little hints. And I didn't push her... You know she was on beta blockers? Feeling anxious."

I didn't.

More new information. More gaps. A widening fissure between us. But no. That's not true – we were close, weren't we? I know we were.

"She told me that sometimes she felt paranoid. But the medication was helping, so she said."

"Paranoid? Paranoid about what?"

"Mum, don't. Please don't. I don't want to... I don't want to talk about this again."

I thought Jack might jump from his seat.

"O.K., sorry, sorry. I just can't believe that she didn't... she didn't talk to me. If that's true."

"If that's true," Tim said, eyebrows raised, fingering the edge of his whisky glass.

"I think she thought, you know, that you had always sort of put her up on a pedestal, mum. That it wouldn't... fit. Like she would have let you down."

"Let me down?" I heard my tight voice, far away. Far away from you again.

"Look," said Tim, firmly. "We don't need to go over all of this. Yes, she was a bit unhappy. But not seriously depressed. Not crazy. At least, no more than I am..." He threw these last words away, towards the table. "No, no one knows all the intimate personal details of her relationship. Yes, she had an accident... She might have been in a bit of a state, too thin, yes, emotional, a bit anxious, and too drunk. But not – she was just – like many young women are. This day and age. You know how it is. You've worked with young people for years. And she didn't take care. She fell."

"Yes." Jack gave a fierce nod.

"She probably wasn't even meant to be drinking with that medication. I assume she wasn't coping. It's painful. Terrible. But..." He shrugged.

I have always hated that expression with a vengeance: 'not coping'. It strikes me as a mask for victim blaming. A phrase often directed at women. If you 'aren't coping,' it means it is your fault. The issue is with you. You are weak; fragile; you don't have the strength to deal with your load.

Not that it's too much – would be too much for anyone to bear. Not that it's external. Not that the situation is untenable.

I swallowed my coffee in one go, and felt the pungent, too-hot liquid graze my gullet and leave its mark.

Chapter 10

Under my black chiffon blouse, I wore a dark red camisole.

It didn't seem right to be in full mourning gear. Not that Nanna was the sort to wear red. Or the power heels I put on – which also proved to be impractical on a church stone floor. But I felt that it was a visual representation of her inner core. Feisty, in its own way. Not obviously. Not on first impressions. But it was there. Plus, yes, I wanted my own armour for the day.

When Jack and I arrived, there were very few people at the church. I've always had a fear of being late to funerals – and I'd spent the early hours that night struggling to find sleep, glancing at the time, wondering if I had slept in, or if the alarm was due to go off. I had a mental picture of the whole church congregation turning around with a collective gasp while the ex-wife walked in, causing a scene. With her dark red camisole, and her arrogant lack of punctuality.

The church was large and clammy and smelt of incense. It sounded hollow and bare as we stepped down the aisle. As it was, I only recognised a couple of people so far who nodded at me and Jack as we took a seat three or four rows from the front. We were half an hour early, but I didn't regret it. It gave me time to settle and prepare myself. We sat in the quiet and listened to the church organ and the whispers of the small congregation around us.

The service was short and well done. It was simple. The music on arrival was a Mozart piano sonata. The eulogy was given by her younger brother, and it was sweet; filled with little anecdotes from her childhood, most of which I hadn't heard before. We smiled, shook our heads, and cried with love, as the best funerals will make you do. I didn't attend the interment, although Jack went along with Tim at the last minute. I was glad of that. And I was glad that I had come.

"Are you sure you are O.K. mum? O.K. to get there alone?" Jack asked, concerned.

On a soft rotation, our roles were shifting and turning, it struck me. He had started to look out for me. And soon, too soon, he would be looking after me.

"I'll be fine, darling. I'm a big girl," I said.

The reception was held in a comfortable, ancient country pub, within walking distance of the church. I strolled there, checking my mobile phone on the way – a message from Jayne, thoughtfully wishing me luck – lots of spammy emails. The air was filled with a cloudy, heavy humidity, which was uncomfortable to walk in. The arch of my instep was hurting from my shoes and my make-up would have run.

By the time I reached the pub, I wanted to go straight to the ladies, smudged and bothered. Once there, I clipped my hair up with the large tortoiseshell bulldog clip I kept in my bag for situations like this. I wiped my neck and hands with baby wipes, my eyeliner with my finger, and applied some powder.

This was the first funeral I had been to since yours. But I had made it.

I touched up my lipstick and decided to grab a drink and sit outside, rather than going straight to the function room and risk having to talk to strangers. It was clammy enough outside; it would be stuffy as hell indoors, at a wake.

I bought myself a sensible soft drink at the bar, after a brief wait amidst locals and funeral guests, and then strolled outside. I went to the picnic bench furthest from the main door. It was the right choice – I enjoyed the air compared to the stale beer and the smell of the old building inside.

Twenty minutes later, the sun had started to break through the morning haze. The air and temperature felt less oppressive as a small breeze started to rise. I decided I had best make my way inside, although I still hadn't seen Jack. I swung my legs around and was about to stand when I caught the eye of the woman sitting at the table nearby. She faltered.

"Catherine?" she said. "I didn't see you there!"

It was Jackie, Tim's half-sister.

"Hi!" I called, surprised. "I didn't know you'd come down."

I walked towards her. Jackie lived in Scotland – east of Inverness if I remembered correctly – with her husband. She and Tim had always enjoyed each other's company, but they were more like friends than siblings; she was fifteen or twenty years younger, plus she had lived away for the last ten years at least.

"I know. Last minute thing. But I always admired Rose."

I nodded. "Yes, me too."

She looked up and over my shoulder. "Here comes my daughter, Tilly," she gave a quick wave, and dropped her voice. "She's a bit… shy."

She made a sort of stiff, one-shouldered shrug, meant to convey a message of sorts.

Tilly stopped several feet away from us. She was a tall, very slim girl. About eighteen, I guessed. She wore heavy foundation, covering severe acne. She was pretty, with round, full features and shiny hair.

"Say 'Hi', Tills," said Jackie. "This is Catherine. She was at the funeral, too."

"Hello," she said. "It's nice to meet you." For some reason, I was surprised by her soft, broad Scottish accent.

"Hi, Tilly. Did you know Rose?" I asked, for want of something to say.

She shook her head, flicking her hair across her cheeks.

"Just moral support for your mum, then," I said. "That's nice."

"Tilly and I have taken tomorrow off. We thought we'd have a look at a couple of colleges."

"Oh, great! You're in the sixth form?" I looked from Tilly to her mum.

"You're repeating the year, aren't you sweetheart? Getting your Highers." Tilly blushed fiercely, so I trained my eyes on Jackie. "It's hard being a youngster these days, isn't it?"

"I know exactly what you mean," I said.

I pictured you, crying in your bedroom, aged twelve, stomach cramps and emotions tearing up your childhood, hauling you into adulthood. I pictured you, withdrawn and quiet at age fourteen, my worries about your lack of confidence. Lack of words. And I pictured you, sitting on the couch with Jessica, laughing at 'Some Like It Hot'. Starting to settle into yourself. But still, it seemed now, enigmatic in so many ways.

Low down in my stomach, I feared I might start reliving, remembering your funeral, your eulogy, your service. No. This would be too much. I had told myself I would not do this. Besides, this was Rose's day.

Jackie and I made eye contact, and something passed between us.

"Shall we go in?" I asked, turning as I did so, to capture them both in my invitation.

She nodded. "Don't forget your bag, Tills," she said as she stood.

Tilly slowly moved forward a few steps, and then reached over for her pink leather handbag. She was still too far way, as if she was reluctant to come any closer to us. She stretched, part graceful, part gangly teenager - and as she did so, the sleeve of her t-shirt rode up, to reveal a series of fresh, angular scars on her arm, harsh and ruddy in the sunlight.

She waited a few moments after he shut the bathroom door. She stood still, silent, next to the handle. She kept her breath tight and small.

He had scattered his flip-flops in a stagger as if they could run away, and she noticed he had left his mobile phone in the room. He had just asked her to check the time. And then he left his mobile phone in the room. In the room.

Was it unlocked? Was the camera on? No. It wouldn't be. Don't be silly.

Don't touch it. No.

The shower started, and the sound of the water's high-pressure needled her skin. She could feel it. Her body was starting to tremor. How could he bear it?

She imagined the bridge of his nose, the filaments of bristle on his upper lip as he lifted his face into the shards of water.

She leapt away from the door, taking two steps further into the hotel room as she turned, twisting awkwardly in a fractured pirouette.

Her bare feet skidded on the tiles as she raced towards the balcony. She could still hear the shower but didn't dare look back – don't look back – as she yanked the sliding doors open, enough to squeeze through.

She was on the other side, one hand stretching around the latch to shut it behind her and lock her out. Quick. Then it was done.

But his phone was there. In her hand. How was it there? She shouldn't have done this. It wasn't hers. Was the camera on? Her forearm was burnt pink, hairs withered and frazzled, skin cracked and dry. Rawhide. And there, in her hand, was the phone. The phone. His phone. No. And she wore her shame like a shroud. Its blackness jumbled with the fabric of her clothes, her soul, her voice, and she could not breathe. She did not cry.

She leant forward, her body arching steeply over the edge. She felt the breeze hit the back of her neck, cool and real. Beautiful. No need to be scared.

And then the phone in her hand buzzed. Yes. Good. This was it.

This was the sign. This was why.

She understood now.

She put her hands on the wall of the balcony. She put her weight onto her palms and pulled her legs up onto the wall, and under her body until she was a curled beetle. Then she pushed herself onto her knees. The breeze hit her shoulders, and her upper arms. It tried to lift the skirt of her dress. It lifted her.

Check the phone. Check the phone. What does it say? What's the time? Is it time?

She pushed herself up with one hand. Rising, unfolding, she could feel it. She didn't need to be ashamed. She should show them what she really was, what she was that she didn't understand, and they didn't know, and she couldn't tell, and she could do it now. She should. They would understand – and then they would love her.

She felt the toes on her right foot touch something damp as she arched further into the air, her foot slipping, sliding again, not broken now, not damaged. Pirouetting. Graceful. They should see. Her left hand broke free of the phone at last, as her body danced on the wall. Danced.

Lifting. Rising.

Flying.

What's the time, Susie? Tell me, what's the time?

And then she fell.

Chapter 11

I felt a mixture of comfort and relief to be back at my flat, with a faint prickle of excitement in the background, knowing this was the week when I would meet Sebastien. Then I could talk about you again.

Travelling back on the train had felt gritty and sticky, even though it was another crisp autumn day. The carriage was busy and smelt hazily of sweat, and there was little space for my bag, or myself. For part of the journey, I had stood, back to the luggage rack. I used to think train travel was a luxury; something leisurely to enjoy with a glass of wine, a book, the view. Now it felt grimy and irritating. It made me think back to you, journeying to see your father, at an early age. No wonder you didn't do it very often.

I pushed the front door of the flats open and checked the pigeonhole where my mail was always left. There was a large white envelope, addressed with handwriting I didn't recognise, amongst the junk and bills.

I let myself into the flat, and noted the stale, fuzzy air. I opened the small double doors that led out into my patio and put on the kettle, kicking off my shoes as I went. I threw away the wilted flowers that sat in a jam-jar on the counter and ran the tap fiercely into the sink to displace the smell of the stagnant water that I poured out.

As the kettle boiled, I tore open the envelope. It contained a thick brochure, made with brown, recycled card and off-white paper. There was a letter, explaining how they had included the information I had requested. I could gain further updates if I emailed them, their preferred method of communication.

It was information about a natural burial service: woodland burials in biodegradable coffins or the scattering of ashes in wildflower fields.

For a moment, bemused, I thought it must have been connected to Rose's funeral. Had I expressed an interest, somehow? Did they have my contact details? But no – I hadn't -- and anyway, Rose's service was traditional. So, it was a mistake, then? Junk mail? But the letter was addressed to me, by name, and opened with, 'Further to your recent request for information…'. I dropped the brochure into the bin, ripped the letter into small pieces and scattered it on top.

I am not a superstitious person, and I am not timid. I don't see the point in terrifying myself with imaginings and worries about the future that may not happen. Real life is stressful and curious enough. I always told you and Jack to live by focusing on things within your control, and to take action where you could, didn't I? Remember? I hope I have lived my life the same way. I have consciously tried to do so.

At this moment in time, I could not know how or why I had received this letter. But I could throw it away. If this was intended to scare me, somehow – and who knew if it was, or was simply a mistake – then the best thing I could do would be to rob them of this power. Get rid of it. Ignore it. Refuse to be meek.

Do you remember when you were small, when we had a neighbour who caused us endless problems? At number 7? She used to watch us from her living room window if we came in any later than 9 p.m. Her room was in the dark, but you could see her silhouette against the nets. Watching. Judging. Your dad used to take as long as possible to extricate himself and our belongings from the car, to annoy her. Sometimes, to my mortification, he even waved and called to her as she hid, silently watching. I pictured you and Jack giggling nervously as he hollered to her.

She was grumpy, and shouted at you both if you made noise anywhere near her house: or at least what she considered noise. In reality, you were playing or chattering. Nothing excessive, as neither of you were rowdy children and besides, you were both too scared of her to let your guard down.

We even believed she had stolen our bin, spray painted her house number onto it; there was a distinctive crack on one side, and it went missing just as I noticed a comparable crack on hers. I tried to keep that from you both, though I had been successful, until Jack and Tim started to make jokes each bin day about it looking 'remarkably familiar'.

Then she started to complain about Mr Biggles going into her garden when there was little we could do about it, and he was the most placid of cats. All he did was sit on the fence at the end of her garden, half asleep. In the end, the pitiful thing was kept indoors for as long as we could bear. Jack had a fear that she might hurt him, somehow. Perhaps that wasn't so far-fetched.

At first, Tim was amused, then infuriated. But after a while, he was the one who started to get nervous. Did you know that? I hope not. I tried to ensure the two of you were as oblivious as possible. Your home should be a haven, and children need to feel safe and secure. Tim phoned the council to express concerns that she was unstable, and a risk. Nothing happened. I told him that she wasn't worth his energy. He could not control her behaviour, only his reaction to it. In fact, perhaps she wasn't even in control of herself. There was something sad about the situation – I always wondered if she, too, was scared. Scared of everything. Scared of life. But he didn't see it that way.

Eventually, her son moved in with her and most of the issues were curtailed.

So. Three things had happened now. Three odd, unsettling things, and worse than cracked bins or requests to keep a cat away. My car being scratched, the graffiti by my doorbell, and now this, funeral information, directed at me. Implying my imminent death, perhaps. Or that I was old. Vulnerable. This was the most sinister and made it harder to ignore.

Was it meant as a threat?

I followed my own advice, to be logical and calm, and focus on what was within my sphere of influence. These things may not be connected, and I had no way of finding out if they were. All I could do was to make myself as safe as possible, watch, and wait. But not dwell.

"It is better to light a candle than to curse the darkness," I muttered to myself as I poured the boiling water on my tea bag. And then, "You insufferably pretentious cow."

I forced a laugh.

***

That afternoon, tired as I was, I went out and bought two bolts - one for the front door and one for the patio doors - and a new light for the patio, with a motion sensor. The patio was enclosed so I had always felt safe, but perhaps I was naïve. Was I? I pulled out my toolkit from the storage in the garden – shed was too grand a word for it – and fitted the bolts myself, working up a sweat but satisfied to find it simple to do. I set myself a reminder to call an electrician in the morning to change the light. I was happy to admit that was beyond my skill set.

While my dinner was in the oven, I popped next door to speak to Toby and Jon, mentioning my car and the graffiti, and asking them to keep a look out for anyone unusual. I didn't mention the burial brochure. I felt foolish enough telling them about the other issues – though they were quite alarmed when I described the car, sweet boys that they were.

For some reason as I spoke, the shock in their eyes, the concern, brought a crack to my voice as I explained what had happened.

I had a shower and changed, feeling pleased to have been proactive and silly for bothering, at the same time.

I was glad that I had changed my sheets before I went away. Going to bed, I relished in climbing onto the mattress – the most expensive thing in my flat – and dropping down into the crisp, fresh cotton, so different to the nasty, grubby train journey I had made that day, and the sweaty, warm work I had done that afternoon. For a moment, I was concerned that I would struggle to nod off, but I was exhausted, and it wasn't long at all before I fell asleep.

Yet I slept poorly, through a headachy night of bad dreams. I was close to the surface, but never quite waking up. I dreamt of you, of intruders, of being chased, of windows smashed. And I knew who it was. I knew the person hunting us. But every time I tried to see them, to clutch their face, their name, the dream would disperse into another, and they would shift away, out of reach, on the periphery.

Chapter 12

When I was forty-two, I developed a niggling lower back pain. I assumed it was from work, which meant I was increasingly sedentary and desk-bound, but when an irregular smear test led to a hospital visit for a colposcopy and a punch biopsy, this back pain had the hallmarks of something more sinister.

I hope you were oblivious to the extent of my illness, but I'm not certain you were. Although Jack was older, he was in his first year at university, and the distance meant he didn't seem to fully register that my time off work and vagueness about scans and operations signified possible danger. But you were there, young, anxious, and I think perhaps you knew. You may not have understood, but you knew.

Receiving the Funeral Director's brochure brought back to me the unpleasant feeling that hung over me during that time. Regardless of any logic, of any fierce determination to treat this as any other illness, I felt embarrassed and sullied. I'm not sure if this had been bashed into me at some young age, or whether it was generated from the reaction of the very few people I told. They broke eye contact, I noticed. They avoided words like 'cervix' and 'smear,' although these were essential to the narrative. They spoke in vague terms and whispers. Most of them would rather not speak at all.

Initially, I was anxious, with butterfly breath when I went to appointments, and a tremor when I answered phone calls or received envelopes – too large for the all-clear– through the post. But I don't think I believed that I was sick because in the vast majority of ways, I felt well. I felt normal.

Yet relatively quickly, after two further scans, blood tests and a chat with the consultant, somehow, we were talking about a total hysterectomy. In ten days' time.

Your father had been with me at that diagnostic appointment. He hadn't exactly insisted, but I had attended everything else alone and it seemed he thought it was the appropriate thing to do. The fact is, I didn't want him there. Is that awful? I feel ashamed to admit it. I wanted to listen, make notes, and cry afterwards, alone. I didn't want to have someone interrupting my thought processes. And I didn't want to have to worry about his feelings, too. I felt obligated to let him come, however, as otherwise it would have been framed as some sort of rejection by him. He wasn't a sensitive or demonstrative man, so if he took an act that he considered to be 'making an effort', he was mortified if this was rebuffed. By this stage in our marriage, we were rubbing along next to each other without great intimacy, and that friction was starting to chafe. I didn't want to risk a rare row. So, I let him come and pretended I was grateful for the offer.

I am a stronger person now.

In the car on the way home, after we had talked about the invasiveness of the operation, the treatment plan, the impact, and the prognosis, he started to talk through some practicalities in terms of looking after you, taking time off work, and who might be able to pop in to see me in the day. Who might care for me. It was several weeks of recuperation post-surgery, and this was what he focused on. Physical aftercare. Physical recovery. This was not what I was thinking about. But I let him talk.

I remember that I tuned in and out of his chatter as he reasoned things through in a chipper manner as a series of issues to be solved. And then once I was 'back on my feet', apparently, this would all be over. We could get back to normal and this worry, this issue, would be behind us. Because I would look the same. And I would be able to get back to being the practical one who made the day-to-day problems disappear.

As we pulled up in front of the house, it struck me that he was comparing the hysterectomy, and my cervical cancer, to the time he had two wisdom teeth removed. And that was the first time I thought that our marriage might be over.

**

I was in the hospital for four or five days. I was on a small pastel-coloured ward with a cracked vinyl floor and lofty ceilings. Sometimes I would lie and count the ceiling tiles, or stare at the large stain that engulfed the one right above my bed. This was what I did to make sure I did not cry, in that strange, cold place with strange, sad women. I was sure I did not belong there.

You came to see me on the second day, and then I told your father not to bring you again. Pale, flimsy, your eyes darted around the ward, taking in drips, buttons, curtains. I couldn't bear your unbrushed hair in its tangled ponytail. I couldn't cope with your confusion. I hope you didn't feel rejected when you didn't get to come back. I tried to ensure that you were so busy that you wouldn't dwell on my absence, calling the mother of one of your friends and clumsily eliciting a sleepover, and ordering Tim to take you out to your favourite pizza place on another night.

Tim came every day, on the dot of visiting time. On day one he had a bunch of carnations, which I suspected he had bought from the hospital shop, though I didn't mind. I was half asleep, still with a cannula in my hand, a strange taste in my mouth, woolly-headed.

"Hi, how are you?" I asked, vaguely.

"I've got a cold," he answered.

I pretended to be even more drowsy than I was after that, so that I didn't have to talk to him, secretly hoping he might leave again.

I was housebound for at least five weeks – it probably seemed longer to you. I tried to play it down, and I told you it was routine surgery that was quite common, but it's hard to disguise an inability to move.

For the first couple of weeks, I was bruised and shell-shocked. You used to make me flasks of tea to put beside me in the morning before you left for school. You'd ask me what book I wanted. You poured me a glass of water. But I noticed this start to slide away after a while, the novelty of my illness becoming a frustration, an annoyance to you, I think. You were young – time seemed to pass more slowly to you.

Your father did his best, I supposed, but it brought home to me some things I had not noted, or perhaps overlooked, until then. From my vantage point on the sofa, I could see into the kitchen. It was a huge palaver to make something as simple as coffee, it seemed. He would talk about it for a full five minutes before he started, and then leisurely, messily, make a pot, pausing in contemplation between each step, hands on hips. He tipped the coffee from the packet into the cafetière, never using the scoop. I imagined the flea circus of coffee grains splattered across the kitchen counters, bleeding and then congealing on a daily basis. I saw how he grabbed a tea towel to clean up any spillages, smearing them around the kitchen surface half-heartedly when he should have used a sponge. I wondered what would greet me by the time I was well enough to clean.

This was just one example, obviously. I would not jack-in a marriage on the basis of sloppy coffee making. But it is at the core of the issue; an illustration of how I felt. And it probably sounds petty. Snippy. Superior, even. But it is the trivial things that form the basis of relationships: both the frisson and the discord. Once they start to grate, and they shift from one category to another, there is little to be done to pull them back. The respect is gone.

Of course, the operation cured my cancer. And so it should: large sections of my innards had been sacrificed to appease the disease. It had not spread to my lymph nodes, so in some respects I know I was lucky. But there was an imperceptible shift in me, at that time. I had not planned on having any more children, but assuming you won't have another baby is not the same as being told it is impossible. Your role as a mother is changed, forever. The clock stops to stay stuck wherever the hands lay. Plus, I had eyeballed a possible future made up of chemotherapy, radiotherapy, or more surgery, or worse. I had even browsed funeral directors and drafted a Last Will and Testament on my laptop. You don't move on from these things with a saunter. They change you. People expect you to be joyous, and relieved. But there is light and shade in the feelings post-cancer, and they are splattered and jumbled together.

I had also had far more time to think than I had in years, bereft as I was of work responsibility, and limited in my ability to contribute at home. And those thoughts showed me that it was time to move on, alone.

He wasn't surprised when I broached it, less than a year later.

Much as I know that it upset you, I believe you weren't, either.

She tried to shut the door, but they were still intertwined, and he had a flip-flopped foot, a hand, an elbow in the way. They smiled into each other's faces; his glasses steamed up by their combined heat, like breath on a mirror. She could see the bridge of his nose and the filaments of bristle on his upper lip. He leaned in to kiss her, and she tasted the sour lager on his breath.

She pushed against the door edge; he squeezed out of the way, shuffling himself around without extricating himself from the embrace.

"I don't want to let you go," he said.

She smiled but looked over his shoulder.

They stood still for a moment until his grip softened, and she stepped away from him, taking two steps into the hotel room as she kicked off her sandals.

He took her hand and swung her arm as they stepped across the tiles to the balcony. He yanked the sliding doors open, enough to squeeze through.

The warm night was oppressive. A soft hum surrounded her – insects, and then behind that, cars, and air-conditioning units. He had one hand on the handle, his other still tight within her fingers, squeezing periodically to tell her he was there. He was there for her. His beautiful forearm: tanned, hairs sun-bleached and frazzled, skin glowing with the sun. She closed her eyes and took in the soft sounds, the soft smell, and the feel of him, clenched, clasping, until she could not feel the tiles on her soles anymore. She could not feel the evening breeze. She could not feel anything but this.

They fell into a tight embrace, and stood together, sealed in a tangle of limbs for a full minute. She felt the comfort and reassurance of him.

"Do you feel safe?" he asked

"Safe?" She teased. "That's a funny choice of word."

"I'm serious."

"I... Yes," she answered. "I think I do. When I'm with you."

"Good."

She turned herself around without breaking the lock of his fingers, until he stood behind her, with his arms around her waist.

"I could stare at this view for hours," she said.

"It will be alright," he said, kissing the top of her head. "Susie, I promise. It will be alright."

She didn't answer. Couldn't speak through the taste of iron in her throat. They stayed still for a full minute, perhaps more.

"O.K., I think you need some rest, babe. And I need a shower. I feel greasy and tired."

"Ate too much, you mean."

"There's no such thing."

He kissed her on the top of the head, once more, gave her a quick squeeze and then stepped away. She knew he wanted her to follow.

"Two minutes," she said.

He smiled, reluctantly, but then went back inside. The bathroom door gaped then crashed against the wall in the distance; she breathed in the warmth of the night and leant forward to try to see the view between the rooftops. In the distance, she could hear low singing through the water of a shower.

She had both arms stretched out, with palms on the little low wall to hold her weight. She could see the brittle wishbones of her wrists, the tendons and veins protruding through the skin on the back of her hands as knotted yarn. Pale blue, white, through the mottled pink of her burnt skin.

Every time she saw it, her narrowness, how delicate she had become, it was a shock.

She had ignored it for weeks. Too many weeks. Until one day he had asked her what it was: why she was so slim these days. Slim: that was the word he had used. Tactful – an accusation wrapped in eggshells. They both knew that he meant skinny. Thin.

Emaciated.

It was true, she had been off her food, tired and unenthusiastic about most things – meals included. And she was nauseous sometimes. But this didn't fully explain it. And it wasn't intentional. It took a long chat to convince him: a long, painful chat where she had confessed that she had noticed other things but hadn't dared to voice them aloud.

"Things? What things? What do you mean?"

At first, excited, she had thought she might be pregnant. It was humiliating to think of this delusion, now. Then after a month, six weeks or so, she started bleeding most days, watery blood, pale and bright. And she realised that no, this was not good news. This might be very bad news.

But still, she had not done anything about it; tried to ignore it as it grew and swelled into a dark spectre from her childhood and all her fears merged into one.

He told her it could be a number of things. Any number. And made her promise to go to the doctor, then and there. There was a part of him that didn't believe, she thought. That suspected she was restricting her food intentionally. And so, she had taken an appointment, eventually, unable to tell the doctor, when she saw him, how many weeks or months it had

113

been since it had begun. And now she had a scan to attend, shortly after they returned home.

She rubbed her hands down the front of her dress, the thin fabric sticking to her damp skin, her palms feeling the unfamiliar bumps of bones and tissue that used to be neatly packaged in comfortable flesh. There was something there, she knew it, and the doctor had known it, too.

She pictured it again, lying on his fold-out bed, his hands pummelling her abdomen: sharp little fingertips dipped into organs and veins. She had flinched. He had paused, twitched his head, almost imperceptibly to one side. Then he had done it again, for a few seconds longer, then pulled her cotton top back down and asked her to get up. His face was an unsettling mix of grimace and grin as he told her it would be best to get her checked, and that he'd be making a referral, straight away.

Straight away.

Better to get this checked.

We don't treat these symptoms lightly.

She heard the shower turn off, and pictured him, completing his orderly routine of drying each limb with care, then his armpits, then between each toe. She had a few minutes alone, that was all.

The chair nearby was uncomfortable and folded even her slight body into a concertina. It would not do. She chanced the balcony wall — it was low and narrow, but she knew that it was wider than her frame. Cautiously, she turned, put her right hand and arm down behind her, clambered onto the tiles and lay flat on her back.

It was surprisingly comfortable. She felt the back of her calves, her lower thighs against the cool surface: the feeling creeping up her legs, her hips, as she pushed further down into the firm, short wall.

She lifted both hands to her stomach, tentatively. She butterflied her fingers in the air above her belly and then held her breath. She pushed down and tried to find what he had found. Tried to sense what he had. But she was at a loss, jabbing, prodding. Hurting. She could feel nothing distinctive; everything felt taut, hard. Perhaps that was the problem.

In her mind's eye she saw her mum in a hospital bed: unnaturally pale, the skin around her eyes crinkled into thin paper. She remembered all the women. Women in every bed. Except one bed. One empty bed. Where was the woman for that one?

She flattened her palms against her stomach and ribs, below her breasts. Her breath came in harsh, little heaves like an untied balloon. She could feel the rise and fall of her ribcage and abdomen and focused on slowing this, bringing the air further down so that it filled the cavity, pushing her stomach further out, as round as it would go. She was so tired.

It will be alright, he said.

Beneath her, she could hear the laughter of a young child, skipping steps around the lower tones of parents. Beside her, somewhere close by, she could hear the melodious tone of a single bird – was it a cuckoo?

The breeze lifted the scent of mint and chlorine up towards her.

It will be alright. Susie, I promise. It will be alright.

She became aware that her feet were cooling, uncovered, heels pushed against something hard and chilled. Her head jerked sharply to the right, as she almost succumbed to sleep, flicking confused eyes open. She needed to get to bed.

She turned to her side and went to stand. Disorientated.

Confused, for a moment she didn't recall where she was, thought perhaps she was slipping out of bed. She didn't understand what was happening. What was happening? She was sliding sideways where there was no ground. No floor. Sideways and off and she was coming off the wall, where there was no balcony. Nothing.

She tried to grab it, but the wall was too wide. and she found her fingers sliding along cold tiles and then lacing the air.

A sea of panic flood her as she realised that she could not stop this. Her body was in motion, propelling over. Tumbling. Rolling through the air. She could not stop.

She cried out. Cartwheeled her arms, her body horizontal, spinning through the air like a carpet, unrolling. Spinning. Twisting. Unfurling.

And then she fell.

Chapter 13

Sebastien asked to meet me at the end of a shift, at his work. He said free cake was on offer. It was a Friday afternoon, and I took the bus across town to the strip of bars and restaurants where The Blue Plate was. It was an up-and-coming area, and not somewhere that I frequented very often. I wondered if you ever did. I couldn't imagine you being much more comfortable than I was, in this type of environment.

The restaurant was a stylish take on a gastro pub, but brighter, more fashionable, and unconventional. As I walked in, I found myself in an area that mimicked a courtyard – trees in enormous pots and a sort of atrium roof window, stone floor and rustic wooden benches, lobelia growing up the trellis and onto the ceiling, breaking free and flourishing, though we were inside.

I was met by a waiter dressed in a t-shirt and jeans. Expensive, crisp. When I said who I was here to meet, he nodded as if unsurprised, and walked me further in, where the room opened up into a large space, and the floor was a mix of carpet and wood, the seating was made up of velvet booths, sofas and chaise-lounges. There were cushions, blankets, and an unlit fireplace – unseasonal but still cosy. In a couple of months' time, it would be perfect. The central section of the floor had been replaced with

117

reinforced glass and the wine cellar could be seen below.

It was late afternoon and there was only one table occupied. Sebastien was with another member of staff, standing close and listening intently, hands clasped together. He saw me from the corner of his eye and smiled, gave a one-handed wave, but then turned back to the waitress and put a hand on her shoulder, with a squeeze.

As I sat and waited, my mind drifted back to the last time I had seen Sebastien, that I could recall, clearly, at least. There were lots of visitors after the accident and over two hundred people at your funeral. No doubt he was there. Perhaps he also came to the flat. But those times were dampened in sea mist to me, indistinct and muffled.

It was less than two and half years since I had last been around him, and aware of it, in normal circumstances, but seeing him here, out of the context of you, it struck me that he was a man. A broad, confident, handsome man. Your friends were forever conflated with your childhood to me. They were all children or teenagers in my mind. I needed to accept that time had passed. They were no longer young people. They were grown-ups grown further than you ever would.

I sat on a plum-coloured sofa and asked for a coffee. A sparrow flitted between the branches of the potted shrubs and trees, ignored by all.

I didn't have to wait long before Sebastien came over and air-kissed one cheek. He was tall and slim but with broad shoulders, and biceps visible through his tight, black shirt.

"I am sorry," he said, his accent thick, attractive. "She has just found out she… has a personal situation… and she must leave us. I don't like to rush these sorts of things."

I waved a hand.

"Don't worry. I've not been waiting long."

"You have ordered a drink?" he asked, indicating the empty table.

"Yes, just a coffee."

He put one arm around the back of the sofa and leant back, calling out.

"Peter! Peter… hey. Come on."

His voice was loud and commanding, terse; as the waiter looked over, Sebastien raised both hands up in the air at him, indicating confusion, and then he pointed one index finger to the table, in an exaggerated gesture. The waiter gave a half-hearted chuckle but immediately went to the bar area.

"You run a tight ship," I said, smiling.

"He is too slow," he answered.

"How long have you had the restaurant?"

He grinned. "No, I do not have this restaurant. I am a supervisor only. Assistant Manager. I have not worked in this industry for very long."

"Oh!" I was surprised, had assumed he was the manager, if not the owner of the place. "Do you like it?"

He released a long breath through his nose.

"Yes, it is interesting. The hours are long, but I do not mind this. It is not so stressful as some things I have done."

Our coffee arrived, with two slices of a three-tiered Victoria sponge.

"Really?" I asked as I pulled my drink towards me, "What's more stressful than hospitality?" I teased.

He laughed.

"Perhaps stressful is the wrong word. Responsibility. Brainpower. It is not difficult and there will be no terrible consequences if we give someone a bad meal. No one will die. Probably." He smiled. "A bad review maybe, but…"

He pulled his mouth down as if this was not a great concern.

We both picked up our cake forks simultaneously and started on the sponge. It was rich, sweet, light.

"You know that I meet Susie through teaching?" he asked.

"Ah… yes. I think I did know that. I had forgotten."

I was unsure if I was telling the truth.

"I only lasted two years. It is a very tough job this. That is real work."

"Yes, believe me, I know." I gestured towards my chest and tapped my breastbone as I swallowed my cake. He nodded.

"What age group did you teach?" I asked.

I tried to imagine him as a teacher, with his spiked hair and impeccable teeth. Perhaps he would be the subject of a few schoolgirl crushes.

"Foundation," he said. "Little ones."

"Unusual for a man," I muttered.

It was meant as a throw-away remark, but it sparked something in him.

"People are very… cynical about male primary school teachers. Their motivation, and whether they are any good." He sounded both sad and irritated. "Especially ones who aren't straight."

That made some sense, in a way, though in my experience it wasn't a disadvantage to be a man in education, especially at primary age. While the vast majority of the teachers were women, somehow most of the leaders were men. Homosexuality, though – yes, I could imagine that causing a few barriers, even today, depending on the school.

We talked for a while about his brief teaching career, how he had met you, and his move into the restaurant industry. His family had a restaurant, which he had long helped out at, and he had worked there for a while after his degree, informally moving up until he managed the place, but he had never imagined himself moving into this permanently and had retrained as a teacher. One year of training, two years of teaching and he realised this was 'a huge mistake.' After that, a brief stint serving in a Michelin-starred restaurant, to pay the rent, had led to a desire to work in hospitality again – but something stylish, exciting, and adventurous. And he was a foodie, it was obvious to see.

"Do you hope to own your own place, someday?" I asked.

"I can't imagine how I would afford this," he said. "But yes, if I could."

"It doesn't have to be like this, though," I said. "You don't have to start big."

"Or pretentious?" There was a laugh in his voice.

I placed my coffee cup onto the now empty plate, instinctively looking over to see if I could pile this onto Sebastien's, too. But he had only eaten about a third of his and was poking buttercream with the prongs of his fork.

"Thank you for agreeing to see me," he said. "I loved Susie very much."

I nodded, taken aback by his sudden ardour, but touched.

"When Jessica told me that you two had met, I felt like I wanted the same. I know this is strange to you, maybe. I think you know Jessica more, yes? But I miss Susie and I think very often about her and what happened."

"Any time," I said.

The intimacy of our shared grief seemed to be hastening our acquaintance into a friendship.

"I can't believe he is now walking around with this girl."

"Daniel?"

I was intrigued by his tone.

"Yes. Him. Daniel. He is... I think this is disrespectful. He is not a good person. I wanted to tell you. Jessica said you had seen him. I don't think you should see him again."

He looked up at me and then seemed to reconsider what he was saying.

"Sorry." He touched his chest. "That sounded wrong. This is not exactly what I meant. I don't know you, really, and you can see whoever you like, I know. Of course. Please do not be offended. But I wonder if you know everything about him and Susie. I do not think this man deserves your time."

I wasn't sure what to say, where to take this conversation next. My throat had constricted, and I could feel my pulse elevated, my heart a tiny racing beat. A mouse beat.

"You sound angry with him," I said.

"Angry? Yes. I hate him."

I hate him.

"Why?" I asked, fearful of the answer. Desperate for the answer. Where was this conversation taking us?

Sebastien looked at me.

"I think we should have another drink. A strong one."

He leaned back again and looked around. A waiter came over, swiftly.

"I will have a glass of Rioja. Catherine?"

"Well, I'm driving," I lied, unsure why. "And... I don't know. Maybe a dry white wine with some soda?" The waiter nodded and stepped away. "This might send me to sleep, at this time of day!" I joked.

Sebastien gave a quick, polite smile but recommended talking.

"Daniel and I... we had an argument on the first day of the holiday and we have never truly made friends since. Friends – I mean, we were never friends. But we were polite before. Comfortable. That has gone.

For that holiday, I travelled with them and Jessica, but the others they came from Gatwick. So, it was just us four for the journey, for the first time we were a small group together. I noticed all of the things he did, and he did not like it. The things he did to try to control her, to push her down."

He splayed the fingers of both hands out on the table, in stars. We both stopped and looked at them.

"The things he did…" I murmured.

A series of images scrolled through my mind. Things. Awful things.

"I told him to… to back off. He must stop this. It was not healthy. And he was very angry." He looked me in the eye. "I don't think he is used to people standing up to him. Daniel is the boss. Always."

Our drinks arrived and I took a large sip of the wine before adding the soda, which came in a dumpy, expensive-looking bottle.

"I'm sorry, Sebastien. I don't know if I'm following you. You said 'things.' He did 'things' to control her. What do you mean?"

I could hear my voice, as not my voice. Constricted. Warped.

"Silly things. Little things but all the time. Always, so that she could not make her own decision or do what she wanted to do. Susie and me, we had arranged to share a taxi to the airport. But the day before, he changed this. We had to meet there, instead. And on the plane, Jessica and Susie were sat together but he made her move and sit by him. He even ordered her lunch for her. Told her what to eat."

He told her what to eat.

"I… I don't know, Sebastien. He loved her. Perhaps he was just protecting her."

I remembered your eating, how he had said he tried to help you to hide your problem. Tried to get you to eat the right food. That made sense. And yet how thin you were. How very thin.

"No, it was more than this." His voice was rising. "I know it does not sound like much but there was more. Little and often is worse than one big thing, I think. Maybe it was so many little things that she did not even notice it herself. You know? They had to have the same things, suitcases, watches, phones, but this was his style, not hers. He was changing her. Her clothes. Hair. All of it.

And you know, he would not let her go anywhere alone. She kept cancelling her plans. I was pleased we were having the holiday so I could actually see her – but it was very hard to get to talk to her. Very hard. You know, when we were at the airport, she went to the Duty-Free with Jessica, and when she didn't come back as quickly as he wanted, he called her and told her to come back. 'No, come back right now!' He told her. Just from a quick trip to the shop – a quick trip across an airport departure lounge! And she did." He looked at me again. "I was there!"

He was stammering, agitated.

"And… and a few weeks before we went, he told her she had no future as an artist. I saw her, bumped into her in town, unexpectedly. I took my chance, and we went for tea, but it was brief. Too brief. And I asked her if she was still drawing or painting, then she said this. That she had stopped because it was a… a… 'pipe dream'. That is what she said. And a waste of time. He had told her, and she accepted it as true. It was time to grow up, she said. This hurt me the most. Because it was not true. It was not true. Her pictures, they were beautiful." He looked at me. "This is not love!"

My head was reeling, I felt myself trying to grasp the things he was saying. He started up again, but I could not focus, take it in. His words were softly formed, and as I reached out to them, they fragmented, and drifted away. They were all around me. Amorphous. Light. Translucent.

But he was still talking, "— she started eating meat, you know. On the holiday. I was furious. You must understand, I eat meat. I love meat!" He smiled. "But Susie – this was important to her. She had not eaten animals for many years. I know she did not want to do this. It doesn't matter what you think yourself, if you agree or not, you must respect these sorts of decisions when others make them. Principles. Yes?"

I was amazed. You had been a vegetarian since you were eleven.

Sebastien's colour was rising, and he took a large slug of wine. When he spoke again, his voice was lower and deeper. He leant in. I did the same. I could smell the tannins, the alcohol on his breath.

"When she died, she fell, he was supposed to be in the shower, right? He said he could not hear anything because of the shower. And you know it was me who banged on the door, told him to come outside. Did you know this? I hammered on the door, and he came, he was in a towel. I remember seeing him there, this look on his face, his skin was pink and hot, and he had some bubbles on his shoulders, here." He waved his hands to indicate, "Like lace. Shampoo. And I told him to come. I told him: 'Come now, you must come quickly. Susie is outside. She has fallen'... and you know what? He turned around to grab his clothes and I could see the back of his head: his hair, his neck, shoulders. Completely dry. Completely."

His eyes were wide, staring into the distance, seeing it again.

"O.K., Sebastien, stop. Please. I can't..."

I was there again, about to slide down. Bending over the edge. The grief. I could fall. I might fall. Again.

"Sorry. I am so sorry, Catherine."

He grabbed my arm and held it tight. I felt the pressure of his fingertips, warm and reassuring through my blouse.

"I just wanted you to know. I... I needed you to know."

I nodded and placed my hand on top of his.

And then we sat together and cried.

Chapter 14

Four days after meeting Sebastien, I felt both unsettled and emboldened. The weather was still unseasonably warm, so I took the bus to the framing workshop that was around six miles from town, in Botshaw village. It was the type of village that had a craft shop, a rather exclusive soft furnishings and furniture store, a health food mini-mall, and a rustic pottery place that rarely seemed to be open. Where did these people buy their cans of soup and toothbrushes? But still, it was a pleasant trip out.

I grabbed the cardboard tube containing the prints and walked to the bus station. I hadn't even checked the bus times, but it seemed fine to wait, or else I could stroll into the park, nearby, perhaps. This was the privilege of being old. I could do what I wanted, to my own schedule. And I needed to shake myself out. There was no excuse not to walk, take a trip, and get this job done.

As it happened, the bus was due to depart in just fourteen minutes, and I only had to wait ten minutes or so before I could clamber aboard. When we were about to leave, a young mother adjudicated a scuffle between her pushchair and the automatic doors, trying to enter with a young toddler on one hip before the driver pulled away. A gentleman across the aisle for me stood to help her, but she had navigated the entrance and steps before he reached her, having done this, it seemed, many times before. She folded up the pushchair and came to sit in front of me.

It is always painful for me to see young mothers, these days. Much as I want to be happy, and glad that others have joy in their lives, I cannot help but feel bitter and painfully sad to think that you did not. This woman was younger than you had been when you died, and yet she was confidently carrying her child, bouncing him, and chattering away, picking up falling dummies and wiping his dribbly chin without breaking away from the saga of how they were off to see Granny that she was relaying to him all the while.

It took me back to thoughts of you as a baby, a toddler. While I am not one to worry for no reason, it seemed logical to me to worry about you both as babies. The fear seemed wholly grounded in good sense. It is not irrational to think of something so small, pristine, and dependent as vulnerable. It is not foolish to be scared of losing something beautiful and fragile. So that was one time in my life when I allowed the anxiety in.

I didn't remember ever being so sure of myself as a mother that this young woman seemed to be. When Jack was born, I sat by his bedside most of that first night he came home, fearful, that if I left the room he might choke. Or simply stop breathing. It seemed impossible to me that this strange growth I had produced could be life-sustaining – delicate and brand new as it was. Tim slept soundly until almost eight a.m., not noticing my absence, and disbelieving when I told him I had stayed up all night.

If ever you slept beyond seven a.m. – rarely did this happen – I would wake with a jolt not long afterwards and pad into your bedroom to check that your chest was still rising and falling. I was not glad of these lie-ins, because they came with grave and terrifying suspicions. More than once, I woke you when I checked on you. But it was worth it, to keep you alive.

Jack was a worse sleeper than you, and that enlarged all the little gaps and holes in my confidence, turning them into wells of fear for him to fall into, just as I started to nod off, or switch off. So often, I would fall asleep sitting up in bed, with a blanket across his legs, that on the one occasion that a neighbour came and took him into the front room while I napped, I woke to find my arms tightly crossed across my chest, holding on to an imaginary, slippery baby who had gotten away from me for once. I think it became a habit then, waking, sleeping lightly, unsettled. One I could never shift, leading to every night since having been broken. I doubt I am the only parent to find that with children came a whole lifetime of disrupted sleep.

I gazed out the window of the bus. The scenery, as we travelled further away from the town, grew greener and bigger as the roads grew narrower in turn. It had been a long time since I had made this journey, and I started to wonder what I had been doing every day in these last few weeks and months. I often struggled to recall what I had been doing, when asked. You and I used to take bus journeys to various sites and towns a few times a year, but I couldn't think that I had done it at all since your accident, and not even in the six months before then, in truth. In fact, I realised, rhe very last time I had done something similar I was alone, as I was this time. And I had bought you a present that I had never had the chance to pass on. A little silver stand for your earrings, with branches and twigs, shaped as a tree. It struck me that the last, long bus journey I had taken was in Crete.

The baby started to fuss, and this brought me back to the here and now.

"You're a greedy little thing, aren't you?" She said, affectionately to him. "You've not long been fed." This was addressed up and out into the bus, by way of vague apology. I smiled reassurance, though she didn't see.

"There's only time for a quick feed now, so that will have to do, Mr Piggy."

She unbuttoned her cotton top swiftly and put him to her breast.

The man across the aisle coughed gently and squirmed, then turned to look out of the window. I smiled to myself. I remembered the panic I used to feel, when I realised that my baby needed feeding, in public. The desire to feed but the anxiety that it might lead to an issue. She did not seem to have this fear. I was glad things had moved on, to some degree, at least.

I was approaching my stop and I pressed the bell and slowly started to walk to stand in the area by the driver. An elderly lady was close on my heels. As the driver indicated to pull over, she asked the young mum if she was breastfeeding, slightly too loudly. She smiled placidly and nodded in return, then looked back down at her child. I pictured you, had you been there, ready to intervene if necessary. I wondered if I should do the same. But there was no call: before she got off the bus, the lady took two steps back to her and held up a bottle.

"Would you like some water?" she asked.

***

I went straight to the framing workshop and ordered bespoke frames for the prints. The staff in the shop dutifully fawned over the pictures and advised me on wood, glass, and borders for the pictures. I chose chunky, white wood frames, thick white borders, and non-glare glass. In the end, the prints would take up a lot more space than I had expected. But it was worth it. They would be ready in about two weeks, I was told. Another trip out, then. Good.

I wandered around the large workshop space once I had been served, marvelling at mirrors, frames, and paintings – unsure, sometimes, which were for sale, and which were ready to be collected by customers. It was a treasure trove. There were mottled, freckled mirrors with heavy brass edges, pre-Raphaelite prints edged in solid oak, and quirky collage frames for family photos – even a frame that appeared to bend at ninety degrees around a corner. By the front door, I spotted a small frame with edges resembling a criss-cross of twigs. Impulsively, I asked one of the staff if it was for sale.

"Ah… yeah. That's only just come in, actually," the young lad said. "I'll double-check the price for you." He took the frame and typed into the till fiddling and scrolling on the touch screen.

"Twenty-five," he said.

"I'll take it."

"Why not?" he said. "Gift wrap? Is it a present?"

"Yes, for my daughter."

The words came out before I even knew I was saying them. Not so much a lie as a memory. A moment from the past.

"I'm sure she'll love it," he said.

Chapter 15

When you were twelve years old, maybe thirteen, we used to go shopping about once every month or two, on a Saturday. We would start at one end of the city High Street (such as it was) break when we approached the end, for breakfast or lunch, and then waddle back, going into any shops we had missed on the other side of the street. I could usually (though not always) talk you out of spending too much time in the shopping centre – with its lights the colour of migraines. We set ourselves a spending limit each time – yours was laughably small, £5 perhaps, coins in a sequined purse. Mine was twenty or thirty, supposedly, but when I added everything up at the end of the day my spending was always closer to £50.

Now, those shopping trips are among my most precious memories.

You were so excited over little things: sparkling nail varnish, tights on special offer. Your fluffiness, and lack of cynicism, was contagious. And you didn't seem to mind being with me or seen with me; your chicken bone legs under baggy leggings; your wavy hair tangled into a bun, of sorts. In the winter, you wore a synthetic, fake fur coat – white. In the summer you wore loose, patterned t-shirts, over tight vests. Your arms tanned and tiny, but sturdy then. You always walked slightly ahead of me, almost skipping, trying to sashay instead, trying to batten down the pre-teen energy that still bubbled within.

I avoided shopping as often as I could, now. I went into the town centre four or five times a year, and two of those would be around Christmas. I hated the way the aircon in summer – the heating in winter – would burn my face and steam up my glasses as I stepped in. I hated the loud, aggressive music. I hated the queues. Carrying the bags to the car, my puckered palms turned to gristle and string.

My trip out of town, and the events before that, had filled me with a boost of confidence to step into out-of-the-way situations again, and I ventured into town to do the shopping I had been putting off for two weeks. I had gone in early, driving so that I could leave when I wanted, and it was approaching lunchtime when I started to head back to the carpark. I had well exceeded my spending limit, of course. I could feel the ants' trail of sweat that was running down my spine from the back of my neck, while my arms rocked up and down as uneven scales from the fluctuating weight of my bags.

"Catherine!" The familiar voice cut through the crowds. "Hey, Catherine!"

I turned to my right and looked behind me to see Daniel standing outside of a women's clothes shop: leather satchel slung low, navy jeans, a tight t-shirt covered by a fashionable cardigan, soft baby blue.

I walked over to him. "Well, this is a surprise."

"I don't usually hang around women's clothes shops, I promise." He leant in to kiss me. "It's Sophie's lunch break soon."

135

"How are you?" I asked.

"I'm… I'm good, actually. What about you? Been anywhere? Seen anyone?"

I had been to Rose's funeral, of course, but instead, I said, "Yes, I've seen Jessica again. She gave me some prints from her exhibition, can you believe? She just brought them around. A gift."

"Oh, wow," he declared and raised one hand to clutch his chest as if very touched. It seemed insincere, but at least he was trying. I could hear my own voice. Flat. Cold.

"I went to Botshaw, to that framing workshop and treated myself to expensive frames for them. You know where I mean?" He nodded but looked vague and non-committal. "And also –"

Daniel's phone rang. "Sorry, sorry, one min… Hello?"

A frown unfolded across his face, and then lifted again. He turned away from me, slightly.

"Right. Well, O.K. then. Shall I meet you there or – O.K. if it is just another five minutes. That makes it… 12:38, then." He disconnected the call and then smiled at me. "Running late, poor thing. Sounds hectic."

"I'll wait with you."

"No, you don't need to do that," he said.

Then he did something odd with his mouth, pushing his lips to one side and jutting his tongue into his cheek. Was he irritated?

"Well, anyway, I was going to tell you that a few days back I saw Susie's friend Sebastien. Remember him?"

136

He looked up at me. Did not speak for a beat.

"Yes, of course, I remember Sebastien."

"You're not friends, though?" I asked.

"Not exactly," Daniel said. "And how is Sebastien?"

He said his name as if it troubled his mouth. Like hot food that he wanted to spit out.

"Well, he's, he's successful and he's well and everything, but... he was a little upset when we spoke about Susie."

I was emboldened. Testing.

"Let's sit over here," he stated, gesturing to a bench on the pedestrianised walkway in front of the shop.

I was glad to have the chance to put my bags down, though irritated that this was an instruction, not an offer – so, somewhat petulantly I suppose, I put my bags on the bench next to him, as he sat. But I stayed standing. Over him.

"Go on then," Daniel said. He sounded weary, bored even. "Let's hear what the little shit had to say."

I felt a jolt, but I smiled. He was not going to throw me off my course.

"He – Sebastien – he was quite emotional about Susie. He misses her a great deal, I think. And he was troubled. He had... concerns about... how she was and how well... you and Susie were getting along. He didn't think the relationship was exactly... I don't know. Healthy?" I said, struggling, searching for words that would keep the conversation going and not give him an excuse to leave. I needed him to stay. To respond.

"Healthy," he said. "Right. What else? I just know there's got to be more."

I looked at him, surprised by his candour. He was letting his side down, emotion getting the better of him. This was a part of him I had rarely seen.

"Nothing specific, it's hard to explain. He was just a bit upset about the whole thing. He implied – he said he thought she'd lost her way. Was changing. Not happy."

"Well, yes," he sounded as if what I had just said was obvious, ludicrous. "We both know she was unhappy. We know she had lost her way. Ha! Well done, Einstein. I told you about the food, didn't I? Her problem. I don't suppose your beloved Sebastien knew about that. He has a habit of putting two and two together and making cinco."

"Does he?" I looked at him, determined to keep my face and voice neutral.

I was rather enjoying seeing him squirm, but at the same time, there was something about this exchange that was undeniably disturbing.

"Yes! Look, Catherine, sit down, would you? Let me explain. I don't want to, to lose you as well. This is all so bloody unfair –" these last words were swallowed in a sob. "Sorry," he said, wiping his eyes, hard.

The tears were real; I wasn't sure if the words were.

"O.K.," I said.

He had both elbows on his knees, sitting spread-eagle. He rocked his feet up and down on the stone paving.

"Catherine." His voice was calmer, deep. "How well do you know Sebastien?"

He looked at me.

"Not a lot... But well enough," I said. "I've met him a few times."

He nodded and looked at the space between his knees. This was mannered. Infuriating.

"And how long have you known me?"

"I... almost three years, I guess – "

"You've met me, how many times?" he interjected.

"I've no idea..."

"Right."

This made me feel ridiculous. He was a clever man. No. That was a cynical thought. He was a hurt man. Or could he be both? It was all too confusing.

"So, think about it, Catherine. I know you are upset – that's understandable – but think logically. Really. Does this sound right to you? Does it add up?"

"I –" I faltered.

"Who should you trust? The man who your daughter loved. Or a man you barely know? Logically? Really? Who can you trust? Don't you think you might be letting your imagination run away with you?"

"O.K. Daniel. You tell me, then. You tell me your version of the story. Why on earth would he say these things? He was her friend. She cared about him. Why would he lie?"

I was momentarily irritated, patronised, and felt the need to fight back. I didn't know what to think, but I didn't like being battered into a corner like this.

"Sebastien is a troublemaker. Always has been. I don't know why – I guess he has a chip on his shoulder because he's a failure. Chucked out of teaching and now basically a glorified waiter. He has always resented my success and made fun of my work in Trust. Talked about me as if I had just landed on my feet. Won the lottery, or something. No credit given for hard work and brains."

"O.K.," I said, for want of something to say.

"He used to make comments about my clothes, my taste in wine – all of that. You know the type…"

I wasn't sure I did. But I nodded. "Go on."

"He had always been a bit jealous of me and Susie. He used to act like she was his sister, if he had some special relationship with her. This little baby sister act: 'my Susie-Sue' he used to call her. It was nauseating. Then in the weeks before she – it happened – he seemed to develop a massive, lusting crush on her. More than a crush. A fixation. Obsession. It was atrocious, especially when it had all been platonic before. Then this comes out of the blue. It was… grotesque."

"A crush?" I almost laughed, "But he's gay!"
Daniel snorted.
"Really? Is he? Is that what he said?"
He shook his head and looked away.

Thinking back, I couldn't recall his exact words, but he had said something about his sexuality. I was sure he'd said he was gay.

"Bi," said Daniel, with air quotes. "Supposedly. A horny bastard, more like. Gets it wherever he can."

I could feel my hackles rising. The laziness of the inference.

"What exactly are you trying to say?"

"Look. Live and let live, I say. He can do what he wants. But he was creeping her out, Catherine. It got to the point that I thought about cancelling the holiday. Really, it was that bad. But Susie said she could handle it, that we shouldn't let him spoil things for us."

I watched his face as he spoke, flickering between staring hard at me, large pupils, curled brows and looking away, to his hands, to the ground. He was a lost young man again, a grieving lover. Loyal Daniel. Dutiful Daniel. And he was. He was that man.

"He wanted to sit by her all the time – in the taxi, on the plane. He scowled at me constantly. He just… wanted me out of the way. It was obvious. But I loved Susie – I wasn't giving up that easily. Not that I thought he could win her, of course. She didn't want him. But I wasn't going to let her get creeped out and mistreated by some frea—"

He paused and steadied himself again.

"Sorry. That's uncalled for," he held both hands up, mea culpa. "Catherine. Please. Just look at me. You aren't thinking straight, and that's understandable. We are all looking for answers to this impossible riddle. But you need to trust me. You

141

used to trust me. Right? And I'm the same person. I'm the same. I am. Don't let some stranger start making you doubt what we have here… we've got a shared history. Think about what you are saying. No one in the world knew that wonderful, beautiful young woman like we did. No one. Not Sebastien. No one."

He lunged forward and grabbed my hand; I felt his cold little fingers needling into my palm. Tapping, drumming through so that my thinking was broken, interrupted by this Morse code. The images flicking in and out. Sebastien standing close, grabbing the waitress' shoulder. Sebastien calling out, domineering. Sebastien telling me not to see Daniel. I hate him, he said. Hate him.

I hate him.

Daniel was right, about one thing for certain, of course. I hardly knew Sebastien. I had no history with him, no prior knowledge. And perhaps he was compelling.

But he was a stranger.

Daniel and I stared at each other, him sitting down, slightly off the bench – almost on one knee - with his one arm reaching out to me. My pose was imperious, but inside I was tumultuous, scared, and confused.

I had to believe him. It was the only thing that made sense.

We remained there until Sophie arrived by his side, and then he dropped his hand from mine to hers.

She tried to shut the door, but she fumbled. He was up close, brushing skin to skin. Hot. Distracting. She was reaching over his shoulder to push the door behind him. Quickly, softly. The filaments of bristle on his upper lip brushed her neck. Sparks.

"Sshhh," she sniggered. "He'll hear!"

Finally, the door clicked shut. She leapt away, taking two steps further into the hotel room as she turned, twisting in a fractured pirouette. Giggling, light.

Her feet skidded on the tiles as she raced towards the balcony, away from the sounds of the water in the shower, the routine, the domesticity, the clean. She could hear him following behind, eager. She looked back over to him, over one shoulder, coquettish, unlike her usual self. Perhaps they would kiss. Perhaps.

She kicked off her sandals, and then yanked the sliding doors open, enough to squeeze through.

She was almost on the other side, one hand still on the handle, and he was there. His hands were there. A forearm tanned, bursting out from his tight shirt, the sleeves rolled up. Glowing with the sun, even darker than usual. Beautiful. Warm. His delicate fingers were searching to grasp her arms, her torso, her clothes.

"Don't," she said. "Slow down."

He did not seem to hear. He grabbed the bottom of her dress and yanked upwards, greedily, rough, a child with Christmas paper. Delicate no more.

"Hey – stop it!"

She pulled free but still he did not look at her - his face set, greedy fingers searching, ham-fisted in the air between them. She was staggering backwards now. Staggering backwards, until they locked together in one at his insistence;

143

his coarse wet tongue seeking hers, his hands pulling at her clothes, not even caring where seams began and ended, ignoring buttons, zips; pushing and tearing until he found skin. Until he found her.

And she tried to cry out. She couldn't cry out. He was on her, over her, heavy and hot and oppressive. Shocking. This was not how it was meant to be. This was not meant to be.

"Please!"

They edged further, meshed into one, jerking, awkward. Until she was up against the low, tiled wall of the balcony.

He pulled away from her face, and smirked, his fingers still inside.

She felt the back of her heels against the cool surface, the feeling creeping up her legs, her hips, as she pushed further against the short wall. It was a brief, fleeting, relief to feel something new; something so different from his hot, sour breath. She was propped on the edge of the balcony. His face was back in hers again, though she tried to snatch hers away. Him, there, forcing his cheeks, bones, mouth forward, hard, brutal, their arms and hands and fingers a confused tangle of limbs, in a mass of flesh against torsos. She could not breathe. She leant back, her body arching steeply over the edge, trying to inch further away, as he lifted her skirt higher.

"Please…"

He yanked his fingers away from her and pulled at his flies, trying to rip buttons from their holes, rushing, frantic.

She felt the toes on her right foot touch something damp; her foot slipping, sliding, then her hand buckling beneath her as her body jerked down violently, and she tumbled backwards. She saw his face — blinking into confusion, flashing into shock.

They both lifted their hands, seeking hands, fingers lacing the air, missing, inept, never touching. Never quite reaching one another.

And then she fell.

Chapter 16

My phone bleeped with a message from Jack before I had fully awoken.

Do you remember the time when she painted my face with lipstick that turned out to be permanent marker? Hip Hop Happy B-day to my beautiful lil sis, Susie. X

This time last year, I was still a raw heap of shock. You had been gone three months, and the calendar seemed unutterably cruel to come around to your birthday so soon. I didn't know what to do and had spent much of the day in bed, sobbing and sweating. Jack had tried to call me so many times that in the end, he sent one of his friends around to bang on the door until I answered with musty pyjamas and an anaemic, unconvincing smile. The poor boy who stood there didn't know what to do with himself. But he was visibly relieved. Jack made me promise never to do something like that again.

I answered his message.

Today, Jayne and I were going to drive to Eccleston village, walk the lanes and perhaps the shops, and then go to your favourite tearoom, Whites. And talk about you, Susie. To celebrate you.

You looked like Barbara Cartland for days x I texted back and then got up to make myself some coffee. While the cafetière settled, my phone pinged with

LOL. Who? I'll Google it later. Love to you, old lady mumster x

I picked Jayne up at 11 am. As she climbed into the car, she was carrying a small, hard-backed notebook, embellished with red flowers.

"Brought something with you, in case the company is boring?" I asked.

"Yeah, something like that." She clipped her belt in place. "No, actually I thought we could press some flowers in it. For Susie. She loved flowers, right? I've put tissue paper in, see?"

She carefully opened a page, and I caught the bright, white rustle of the thin paper. I didn't say anything.

"What do you think?" she asked.

I was pulling away into the traffic, looking over my right shoulder, but I could feel her eyes on me, head turned my way, trying to seek my answer.

I straightened the car up and drove forward.

"I think you're a great friend," I said.

***

On the way to Eccleston, Jayne chatted away about a work problem involving a colleague who had lost their cool with a parent at the school. Her impressions, and the ridiculous insults he had used all made the story more amusing than it might have been. The student apparently wasn't doing any work in class, or homework, which the parent inferred was simply because it was 'not stretching' for her and 'boring'. The teacher had become so infuriated he

147

had asked the father why she chose to stay at the school rather than take up her place at Cambridge University. At one point, I had to ask her to stop talking so I could safely navigate a roundabout without crying with laughter.

"Anyway, I know I'm being flippant. But it's actually quite stressful. He's a great teacher… just a bit of a —"

"Twat?" I finished.

"I was going to say maverick." She laughed. "Sorry for going on. You must have loads to fill me in on, too."

"Not at all. I mean, you aren't 'going on.' I need the distraction. This is real. I suspect a lot of the stuff I've been doing lately is… less so."

"That sounds intriguing," she said. "Like what?"

I thought of the graffiti by my doorbell. The funeral brochure. I didn't want to; tried every day not to contemplate what they could mean. And there was no point dwelling on them. No point. No. Nothing I could do.

I gave my head a shake.

"Well, you know I've seen Daniel. He came around — I told you, didn't I? Last week I bumped into him in town, as well. We had a sort of run-in, I suppose you could call it. And now I feel like a stupid old woman. Not accepting the truth. Looking for a villain."

"You mean with Susie, right?" she asked.

"Yup," I said. "Again."

I told her about the meeting with Sebastien. How he was alluring, compelling, but perhaps there was

148

something 'off' with him. I hadn't thought it at the time, but well, maybe. I didn't know. Daniel could be right. How could I know? And then Daniel explained it all away. And really, what is more likely? A strange conspiracy theory sold to me by an attractive Spanish man who I hardly knew; or the explanation given by the man she lived with? The one the police believed, too. She listened as I talked through my thoughts, my conversation flitting and ducking, chains of words, starlings at twilight.

"I know it's odd and frustrating, and… and confusing, I guess. But the simplest explanation is probably the true one," she said, almost to herself, flicking the edges of the book in her hands.

"She was delicate. But she was strong, wasn't she? She would have looked after herself – stood up for herself, I mean?"

Jayne nodded, though she didn't speak. I heard the creak of her leather jacket, and a faint jingle from her earrings.

"Jayne," I said, louder. "If it was true, what Sebastien is implying, or accusing, even… she wouldn't have stayed, would she? Not Susie. I mean, I know that people do. And they are trapped. Or feel trapped. I'm not judging – God, please don't think that – I understand." I glanced over to her, then back to the road. "Some people are completely trapped or duped, and they make themselves essential to them, these men, or these… people, maybe. They make themselves seem like the only option. So, people with no resources, no family, no… capital of any kind. They stay. They think they have to. Or maybe they do have to. Literally. Because they have nowhere to go. And... that's awful."

"Absolutely," Jayne said. "It happens."

"But she did, didn't she? Susie. She had other options. She had me. She had her brother. Education. A job. Self-esteem. Christ, it turns out she even had her bloody dad! Why would she have stayed if that was true? That's what I've told myself. Basically, what Sebastien is saying doesn't make sense. So, it can't be true. It can't be."

But Jayne didn't say a word.

***

The tearoom looked almost the same, though the walls had been painted a fresh light green, and perhaps there were new tablecloths; I couldn't be sure. Our walk had been gentle, meandering. We had strolled down the lane that came off from the carpark, lined with hedgerows that later turned to wire fences. We thought we knew where we were, having taken this walk three or four times before – at least twice the pair of us had walked it with you, I was sure – but somehow, we ended looping back towards the village, rather than out towards the church. I didn't mind. The air was moist and chill, refreshing, but the watching rain hung heavy in the textured sky, threatening to start at any minute.

We sat near the window and ordered scones and tea. Jayne was fiddling with the few flowers we had found, trying to ensure that they sat nicely between the pages.

"I'll put it between two heavy books when I get home," she said. "We can get it out next year and see what they are like. We could add to it, then, if you like?"

"Thank you."

I was tearful for the first time that day, touched by how thoughtful she was being, and bleak that you would still be gone, still lost, this time next year. A whole year further away from me. Would I know more by then? Would I be at peace?

Our tea arrived and I was glad of the heat through the china cup, bringing me back to here, now. I glanced around the room.

"Susie always loved the strange little fairy pictures here," I said. "Nymphs and elves. It was one of the reasons she fell in love with the place. I'm glad they still have them, after all this time… I suppose that sort of thing often appeals to children. Small creatures with unexpected powers."

"Look at that one," Jayne said. "It's almost gothic looking. It's very dark. A rather strange choice for an English tearoom, no?"

"To be honest I never looked that closely. I always thought them twee."

"Hardly," said Jayne. "That's a selkie. They are half seal, half human. Beautiful women who can morph from one to the other."

I stretched myself up, and reached, almost touching with my index finger.

"Really? But she looks like she's in love," I said. "She looks like she's running away with that man. He's carrying her sealskin for her, isn't he? Almost like a coat over his arm. Like a gentleman. It's odd, but in a way it's lovely."

Jayne frowned.

"I think," she said. "If I remember correctly, selkies lost their freedom when men took their skin from them, trapping them in human form, forever. Then that meant they had to stay on the land. It was a way of... sort of ensnaring them. So, he's not exactly doing her a favour, there."

"Not so lovely then," I murmured, bringing my hand back down to the table.

"Not so lovely after all."

***

I was pulled from my sleep by a thread, lifted up, and slammed down. Confused at first, I realised that I was home. In bed. And my mobile phone was ringing. My alarm clock told me it was 1:24 a.m.

Jessica's name was on the screen.

"Jessica?" I answered, my voice thick with sleep and dehydration. "What's wrong?"

There was a sob at the other end.

I flicked on my light.

"Jessica, tell me. What is it?"

I sat up, groggy, my mind speeding up, waking up, rushing through scenarios.

"H... Hi," she stammered. "Catherine?"

She sounded confused – as if I had just called her. As if she was the one awoken by the phone.

"Yes. What's wrong? Tell me. Has something happened?"

"I think it's my fault. The fault. Mine. I think it is. It's..."

She was drunk.

"No, baby, no. It's not your fault. She fell. You weren't even in the same block at the hotel."

It was clear what she was talking about.

"You don't know. You don't."

I heard her take a deep, messy swig from a drink.

"I'll tell you what I do know. Daniel was in the shower. No one else was seen in the room. She fell. It's no one's fault."

Did I know that?

"You don't know what I did, though. I never told you what I did."

I sat up, alert.

"What? What didn't you tell me?"

"For one thing, I left her all night. All bloody night. I didn't even try to talk to her again after he made her sit down. I should have tried. I should... I gave up. And Catherine... I – I got stoned. I left her at the table, and I went off. I smoked a heap of weed. Like some shitty stupid teenager. All holiday, really. Well, most of the holiday, I did. Left her. I was drinking and sleeping and smoking. And she was – she was... I am a terrible person. I should have paid attention."

My heart sank. These details made no difference. The plot was the same. The ending was the same.

"No, Jess. It doesn't change a thing. Honestly."

She lowered her voice. "That's not all. I gave her a spliff. When she left. I put it in her little handbag. I gave it to her. I've been thinking, Catherine, and

153

that's what made her fall. I can't stop thinking it. Maybe she had it and she got smashed on her own because of me and then she went over the balcony…" Another sob, then another swig came down the line.

"The toxicology reports didn't show any drugs. Remember? Only alcohol. Jessica, you're upset, you've had a drink. I don't think – "

"If I'd been a good friend I would have been nearby. Not high. I could have saved her. Maybe I could have. You don't know."

"No. She had a skull fracture, internal bleeding, an ankle fracture, broken ribs, and… the rest. No one could have saved her Jessica. No one."

"But no that's not what I mean! She didn't need to fall. I should have tried harder… I didn't… Oh. Catherine. I'm sorry. I can't explain. She was away from me. And I let her. I let her get away. I can't... I shouldn't have called. It's late. Bye. Sorry. So sorry. Bye."

Then the phone went dead.

Chapter 17

I came back from the dry cleaners to find a handwritten envelope amongst my post, with a black wax seal on the back.

I had gotten up early to collect my purple dress. It was the Stockton Gala that evening, so I had a leisurely stroll to get some air. I did not enjoy going out to such events, so took my time with my preparations, too, and had a slow, relaxed day, building up to the night – hoping dread would mutate into anticipation. Jayne was my plus one, so at least if small talk and schmoozing failed, I could sit and chat with her. I had spent enough money on the tickets – I was determined to enjoy it.

I always felt some reticence now, when I saw unfamiliar envelopes in the post, wondering what could be next. But no, the card transpired to be from Daniel: an invitation to his 30th birthday party in December. I stared at it for a moment, taken aback, and then stuck it on the fridge under a magnet. I would have to park that thought before it led to upset and confusion. Today was not the day.

I made myself some brunch: wanting to stock up on carbohydrates and fluids to try to avoid any overindulgence of wine or sore heads in the morning, and then I settled in front of the television with a thick, cold hair treatment on my head and a warm cup of tea in my hand. I had a deep bath planned, and then late in the afternoon, I was being visited at home by a nail technician. Quite decadent.

There were a couple of evenings when we had done similar, you and me. I'm not going to romanticise things, pretend that we spent every Saturday night sitting together wearing face masks and cucumbers, but there were two or three times when you had come around to the flat and we had a takeaway and painted each other's nails. And we did once spend an afternoon trying out beauty freebies that your colleague had given you, laughing at the names and prices of the products. Those sorts of scenes might be stereotypes, portrayed in magazines and on rom coms, but in reality, I didn't have anyone I could share moments like that with now, and I wasn't sure many of my female friends did, either.

After my bath I nodded off on the bed, the rarity of the bubbles and candles I had used sent me into a deeper sleep than I recalled having in months. I was awoken by the hammering of rain outside, the wind jostling the window in its frame, desperately. It was comforting to be under a blanket, drowsy in the daytime, feeling safe and warm in contrast to the fractious, building storm outside. I drifted in and out of sleep for a while, happy not to wake too quickly. I pulled the curtains apart and lay back down, watching the swarm of leaves and litter that flew by periodically. It was moments like this when I truly appreciated living alone.

After a full thirty minutes of staring at the kaleidoscopic storm, I needed to stir and get ready for my nails. I put on some pyjamas that could pass as 'lounge wear' and turned on the lights and put the kettle on. Grit and rain continued to drum on the window, and I felt briefly guilty to be bringing her to my home and frustrated that the weather was like this on a rare night out.

When she rang the doorbell, ten minutes late, I found the nail technician shivering in an oversized coat, her face drowning in a large hood that emphasised how dainty her face was. She looked young.

"My goodness, come in!" I said, jumping back.

She smiled. "Sorry I'm late, I was trying to park nearby and ended up having to circle around a few times. I'm Eve, by the way."

"Yes. Don't worry. Come in, come in!"

She set up at the kitchen table while I made herbal tea.

"Any idea of colour?" she asked.

"My dress is purple," I said. "So, something dark pink, maybe?"

"Have you thought about black? You could have silver or some nail art on your ring finger."

"You know what?" I replied. "You choose. I'll just end up playing it safe, otherwise."

As she filed my nails and tidied my cuticles we chatted about her business and her hopes of opening a small salon someday. She worked for herself and was glad of this fact.

"My little brother lives with me," she said, seeming both proud and embarrassed at this revelation. "There's not much financial help, not really, so I need to work as hard as I can and think about ways to build on what I'm doing. He's clever. He's bound to go to college; maybe university, even." She beamed.

"Wow, well, that's quite a lot of responsibility for you but it sounds like you are up to the job," I said. "How old is he?"

"Thirteen."

Thirteen. I didn't dare contemplate what they had been through, these two young people, hanging onto each other, finding their way through the mess. Alone. It was admirable. I enjoyed having her here; spending time chatting with someone bright and new. Young.

"Do you have a card?" I asked. "A business card. I can pass some on to people or stick it up in the café nearby if you like?"

"Yeah, I'll give you a few when I leave. Thanks. That's really kind of you."

"I got your number from my friend, Jayne," I said. "She said I would be lucky to get you for today as you were so popular these days."

"Jayne?" she asked. She shuffled in her seat and scratched her ear.

"Jayne Hilton. She's a teacher. Short hair."

As I lifted my hand, I noticed a small cringe flicker across her face.

"Oh, yeah. I do know her. I haven't done her nails in a while… Oh, you need to pick a hand cream!" She pushed three tubes toward me. "I can give you a sample of whichever one you choose."

I nodded, still watching her face, trying to interpret her awkwardness.

Something large crashed against the glass, making us both flinch and jump. For a second, it sounded like someone was ramming the doors. We stared at each other, equally lost. Adrenalin pounded in me, but I also felt an instinct to protect her, this young girl. To keep her safe.

"What on earth was that?" Eve said, her voice a pitch higher. "Did it break the glass?"

"No, no. At least, I doubt it… I hope not!"

I laughed, nervously, getting up to go over to check. She stood up and turned to watch, edging towards me and the curtains, staying a step or two behind me.

I pulled back the long sheer curtain that covered the left door and felt myself recoil backwards, my spine curving like a cat. I heard her sharp intake of breath, close to my left ear.

The glass was smeared with blood that ran down from head to knee height in a violent paint-stroke of crimson. I followed it down to the ground, still holding the curtain in one hand, gripping it like a handkerchief, or a favour, for luck.

There on the doormat was a large, dead crow, its head almost severed from its body, resting at a right angle, in a pool of near-black blood.

Chapter 18

The function room was striking: the ceiling had been draped with indigo cloth, and pinpricks of light popped through. The tables and chairs were plain white with huge displays of hydrangeas – lilac, dusky pink – in the centre, and trails of palm leaves crawling out and creeping down the tables towards the floor, almost hitting the ground. Battery-operated tea-lights dotted the tables between the plates and glasses, effective in the low lighting of the room. I had been to this hotel before, and this far exceeded my expectations. It was unexpectedly lovely.

Jayne and I sat at a table with two of the school governors and their partners, only one of whom I knew. To my right, was an ex-colleague of mine, Ellen, who had also retired now, and had attended with her husband. I was grateful for the thoughtful placing, which meant I didn't have to make too much small talk, as there would be dozens of people from the local business community in the room, sponsors of several school events. I had never been good at talking local politics, business, and finance, and often felt myself bobbing along through the conversation, scared they might notice I was adrift.

Your father had always been skilled at that sort of thing, and it was one of the ways I missed him when we first split. It's shameful, but it was one of the only issues, perhaps, I needed him for. At any event or gathering, I could stand by him if necessary and somehow benefit from his conversational skill with strangers and acquaintances. I could hold his arm, and say nothing, but smile, graciously. I would be considered a good conversationalist by association. He had a way of asking gentle, nudging questions that allowed the other person to continue talking about themselves without feeling they were dominating the conversation. He seemed so interested. And yet he told them little of himself. Strangers love that sort of thing – life partners find it infuriating. I could not do this when I meet people. Still cannot. I am either very quiet; mind blank; feeling awkward – or I talk too much and am far too candid. There is no in-between, it seems. Or at least, that's how it feels.

The food was tolerable for a large function, and there was a range of entertainment throughout the evening. With each sketch or turn, buckets were passed around the room. They opened with a dance performance, very professional but also amusing when one of the P.E. teachers joined the young people at the end. During the starters, an amateur magician – an ex-student? – performed close-up magic at the tables. As a highlight, there was a serious piece of drama which almost worked, written by an ex-student, plus speeches between the main and dessert. Jayne was beaming. During coffee, a band comprising sixth formers entertained us with 60s and 90s rock, and indie classics. I needn't have worried about small talk, as there was little chance to speak.

After the band had finished, a local DJ came on, and Ellen came back from the bar with a bottle of Prosecco, while Jayne circled the room, dutifully.

"Well, I won on the scratch cards." She indicated the bottle. "So that's basically free money!"

The school committee had taped lottery tickets to the bottom of our chairs and told us to check them as we were seated.

"Shall I?" she asked, ready to pour into my glass.

"Go on, then," I said.

I had drunk little, swept up in the nostalgia of watching young people perform and not feeling this was the place to let my hair down too much.

"Cheers."

We clinked our glasses together.

Ellen and I chatted at a level that dropped in and out of intimacy, the frequency shifting up and down. We had known each other a long time, and she had been supportive after the accident, but we had never been very close friends outside of work, and I hadn't seen her in at least 8 months. It is odd how some relationships can stay confined to the workplace like that; does it mean you were never truly friends? Or is it just life, perhaps? There isn't enough time for every acquaintance to develop and take a part of your life, take up space and time.

She told me about her oldest son, dropping out of university – or as she hoped, taking a pause on his studies. It sounded extraordinarily messy. I empathised and told her how he might come out the other side, filling her in on Jack and his move to Wales.

She grabbed my wrist.

"How are you doing?"

"I'm… O.K.," I said. "Thank you."

I smiled and took her wrist in return. We were briefly locked in a net of limbs.

Her husband came over, tweed jacket on, red wine in hand.

"What's all this?" he asked. "I strongly disapprove of maudlin conversations on a night like this. You know what I do approve of? Wine!"

He topped up our glasses. Ellen broke free of me.

"You remember Catherine?"

He stuck his hand out to shake mine, though he didn't answer. I wasn't sure if we had ever met or not.

"Pray, how do you know my lovely wife?" he asked.

He leant across her to talk to me, and she had to lean back awkwardly in her chair.

"We used to work together," I said. "A little while ago, now."

"She was the big boss," Ellen said.

"I see."

He raised his glass with a small toast of sorts and took a large swig.

"We were just talking about Tom's disastrous second year," Ellen interjected.

He dropped one arm on the table and rolled his eyes.

"That's ten grand we'll never see again. Fifteen, no doubt. But as long as he gets to cut politics, everything will be alright. Heaven forfend he should have to stick at something…. Tell me you don't have any teenagers knocking about the place, Catherine? They're tougher than babies."

"How would you know? You didn't even change a nappy," Ellen muttered.

She caught my eye and winked.

"Not anymore," I answered. "My son is now a responsible grown-up. He's a manager in the care sector."

"Very good, very good. You obviously thought that one through. No excuse to squirrel you away to a home in a few years, eh?"

A few years. But I smiled, dutifully, for Ellen's sake. I felt myself shutting down, unable to think of what to say. Ellen began to fill in the gap at the same time as her husband spoke again.

"Catherine's son is— "

"Just the one then?" he asked.

"Sorry?" I asked, turning to Ellen.

"Just the one child?" he answered before she had time to speak.

I dreaded this question. I always wanted to say no, I had two. I have two. Whatever answer I gave, unless it was a blanket lie, there would always be follow-up questions.

"I also had a daughter. She died last year."

"I'm so sorry to hear that," he said. And it was the first sincere thing he had said, it struck me. He crumpled. "Young, was she? Was she sick?"

Ellen put a flat hand out towards him, not quite touching, indicating enough, stop.

"No… she had an accident."

"Catherine's daughter fell while she was on holiday," Ellen said and gave him a pointed look.

"Ah, I remember. Yes. Christ… That's really shit."

For once, I was glad of his candour.

"Yes. Yes, it is. Truly and utterly shit," I said.

We tapped our glasses together and then he leaned back in his chair.

**

Jayne and I were talking over a second, cold coffee when Ellen's husband appeared again by my side. His lips had a bruised tinge, and he was drunker than before. I'd already mentioned him to Jayne, and she clocked him, instantly.

"Catherine! Ellen's just told me who your girl's young man was!"

"I'm sorry?" I asked, sipping my coffee, for something to do.

"Dan Fitzgerald. Dan the man! He was going out with your… your…"

"Susie," said Jayne, blatantly irritated.

"Susie! Yes. Dan and Susie, then. Well, I never."

"You know Daniel?" I asked, superfluously.

"I was his boss when he was a youngster. His first job from uni. Quite the highflyer. Lovely lad! Lovely."

"Yes," I said. "If I see him, I'll tell him you said 'Hi'."

I started to turn back towards Jayne. I didn't want this now. But he leant down conspiratorially.

"Good-looking lad, eh? I bet they were a handsome couple... Yes, Dan. Such a good chap. Such a good chap. I'm so glad to hear your daughter had a good'un, as they say."

"Well, it's a small world," muttered Jayne.

"Do you know, I saw him a couple of months ago!" he declared as he recalled it. "Not to speak to – driving, you know, but I waved. He was crossing the road with a young..." He trailed away as it dawned on him what he was saying.

"Yes, apparently he has a new partner," said Jayne.

"She's called Sophie," I told them both. Irritated, wanting to shut this down.

"I suppose that's a bit... Well. But then it's been a while, right? A few months, anyway. So... Boys will be boys!"

I blurted out, "Boys will be – "

Ellen arrived at that moment with her husband's coat, pulling faces to indicate sorry and pummelling his arms into sleeves. She would have been even more embarrassed had she known what he had said.

"Dan the man..." he muttered, as he moved away.

We watched them walk across the dancefloor together, arms, belts, and sleeves around each other as a nest.

"He seemed nice," said Jayne, deadpan. I laughed.

"Boys will be bloody boys. I hate that expression. As if it's perfectly understandable if their testosterone holds more influence than their brain. And it's pretty insulting to men, too, if you think about it. Like that's how bloody low our expectations should be."

Jayne gave a tight smile.

"It is weird, though. To think of him with someone else. It's not even especially quick. Not exceptionally. But if I find it weird, I can't imagine what it's like for you."

"Yes," I said. "But to be frank, right now I'm more bothered by the fact someone was singing his praises. And I know I shouldn't be. I mean, he really liked Daniel, didn't he? Why should that be so bloody annoying to me? I definitely would have preferred it if he'd told us some embarrassing story about him being shit at his job, or something, God, when will I move on from this... these... doubts? The blame game."

"I have to be honest," Jayne said, quietly. "Perhaps you never will."

Chapter 19

There is no word for a parent who has lost a child. Unlike widows and orphans, we are nameless. A shadowy group left scattered as individuals, not unified. Unclassified. Some people have told me this is because of its rarity, that we shouldn't need one - and yet since you died, I have met many people whose children have passed away. I must have met many before that time, too, but now realised that I had not taken note, or I had ignored it, or not wanted to contemplate it, perhaps.

Two of my good friends, in fact, had lost children. One had lost a three-year-old boy (Tommy) to a mysterious, intense fever, and the other had lost a baby who had lived for less than a day (Faith). I had rarely spoken to them about it: a fact which only struck me after you were gone. So, I had been complicit in this pretence, too. Because it is not that rare. Not as rare as it should be.

I think, instead, that there is no word because no one would want to speak it.

Ellen's husband's question rang in my ears for days after: "Just the one child?" I vowed to find a way to answer this in future that didn't diminish your memory.

I was reading the newspaper and eating breakfast at my favourite café when I saw Daniel and Sophie, again. It seemed strange to see him here, intruding on my space, uninvited. I was making an effort to get out and about, to appreciate my time and my surroundings. This was not what I had in mind.

"Catherine, are you following me?" He laughed. "We hardly see each other for months and now you're everywhere I go!"

"Hey, sunshine. I think you'll find I introduced you to this café, actually."

He kissed my cheek.

"Rumbled. And now, I'm introducing Sophie to it. It's her sort of place. And I'll take all the credit and be seen as a marvellous boyfriend with fabulous taste." He turned to her. "Grab that table, Soph, and I'll get us some drinks."

He indicated the table next to mine.

She sat down and pulled her woollen hat off. As she did this, her face now in profile towards me, I spotted a large, fading bruise on her forehead: blue against the youth of her skin, with a sticky, striped graze.

"Oh, my goodness!" I said, putting my fork down. "What happened to you?"

She gingerly lifted a finger to the lump.

"It's... I... Well, it's not as bad as it looks," she answered. "It's come up quite dark now, but it wasn't serious."

"I don't know about that; any head injury is a worry." I was especially sensitive to head bumps and bruises these days, always aware of what could be going on beneath. "Besides, serious or not, it looks sore."

She leant forward and nodded towards my plate, with the remains of my breakfast burrito.

"That looks good."

Daniel came back with two hot drinks.

"She's eyeing up your breakfast there, is she? There's me thinking I might just get away with buying coffees. Oh, I've realised I didn't offer you a drink. Catherine. Can I get you anything?"

I swallowed the last of my burrito and shook my head.

"Yes, she's eyeing up a Mexican brunch, but I was eyeing up that cracking bruise on your lovely girlfriend's forehead. Quite impressive." I turned back to Sophie. "You didn't tell me how it happened."

"It was just a silly mistake."

Daniel sat down.

"She's a bit embarrassed about it, aren't you Soph?"

He leaned in and wrapped both his hands around her right hand.

"Really?" I said.

I had a feeling that I had to persist if I wanted to know the story. And I did want to know the story.

"Do tell."

"Drunk as a skunk," he said, grinning at her.

She looked at the table.

"You don't drink, though, I thought?" I said. "Special occasion?"

"Sort of," she muttered. "I actually didn't have that much. But I'm not used to it." Her voice was small and high

"She tripped down some stairs. All two of them."

Daniel took one hand away and brushed her hair away from the graze, delicately.

"Did you hurt anything else?" I asked.

I could feel my heart speeding up.

"No, just the head. Well, and my pride," she said. "And I guess my digestion. I was so sick the next day. I still felt crappy the day after, even. I don't know how people do that sort of thing weekend after weekend. I guess I'm pathetic. Only the second time in my life – the other time I was about fifteen. You'd think I'd know better by my age."

"Don't we all," I muttered, eyebrows raised. "But you're allowed one mistake."

She smiled. "I know everyone says it, but I shan't be doing that again. It's not worth it."

I tried to picture her, this young, unassuming girl, crashingly drunk and falling down two stairs. I saw her hanging off bannisters and twisting ankles. I heard her wrist crack with the full force of her body weight, buckling it. I saw her landing on her knees or jarring her hands. I saw her slipping and bouncing on her coccyx down the steps. But I couldn't see her landing on her forehead and nowhere else.

Daniel looked at me. "What's the matter?"

I must have been frowning.

"Oh, sorry. Nothing. Just bad luck, that's all. And to be honest, many of us never learn – not one hundred per cent, anyway. Not that I make a habit of sliding downstairs, you understand," I laughed. "But hangovers? Sadly, I'm not sure I can promise those days are behind me.

171

"But I'm sorry to hear you bashed yourself, Sophie. Hardly seems fair when you've been sensible all these years," I said, turning to her.

She was gazing at Daniel, a faint grin on her lips.

"Well, that's me done. I can't eat another thing," I said. "Thoroughly recommended, though!"

I waved vaguely at the blackboard as I started to get up and collect my things together.

"You're off?" Sophie asked, surprised.

"Yup. I've been here hours… Bye, Sophie," I said, as I twisted between our two tables. "And Daniel. See you soon, no doubt."

Daniel was sitting back now, legs splayed, hands on calves, content, still looking at Sophie.

"Oh, Catherine," he called, just after I had walked by, "Please don't forget my party."

She tried to shut the door, but the handle slipped between her fingers as they trailed in the air. He slapped her away, like swatting a wasp, and then double locked it. She wanted to concentrate, focus; she could see the bridge of his nose, the filaments of bristle on his upper lip that she had not noticed before.

She turned away from the door, taking two steps further into the hotel room as she turned, twisting inelegantly, a fractured pirouette. She went down; the tips of her fingertips touched the floor, broke her fall; they bent backwards, and then her whole palm slid onto the tiles.

On her hands and knees now, she stayed there for one moment — a sprinter in the starting blocks — then slowly toppled sideways to her left.

She sat, splayed, on the floor.

"For fu- get up." He spat.

She pulled herself up by grabbing at the sheets of the bed, climbing up the footboard of the frame, sliding the bed from its position and leaving the bedding in disarray. She slipped as she reached upright and thought she may fall again.

He grabbed her upper arm and heaved her to a standing position, his fingers indenting in her flesh like dough; the nails of his index fingers piercing through the skin.

She cried out, involuntarily.

"Shut it!" he said.

He let go and turned away. Her bare feet skidded on the tiles as she stepped towards the balcony, unsteady, seeking fresh air. The bathroom door gaped then crashed against the wall: she heard it, didn't dare look back — don't look back — as she yanked the sliding doors open, enough to squeeze through. She heard the shower come on.

173

She was almost on the other side, one hand still on the handle, the other stretching and curling, seeking the latch to shut it behind her once she was through.

But he was there. His hands were there. A forearm burnt pink, hairs withered and frazzled, skin cracked and dry. Rawhide. Large fingers, abnormally large, were fumbling through the gap to grab her arms, blocking her way, until she could not feel the doorframe anymore. She could not hold anything.

He pushed the doors further open and stepped through into the warmth of the night.

"What the hell are you doing?" he asked.

She could feel the damp warmth of his words on her skin. He smelt of garlic, lager, cologne.

She shook her head, scared her mouth would fail to form the words she wanted to say.

"I told you," he said. "I told you; you can't handle your drink. Yet here we are…"

He kept hold of her with his right hand and waved his left arm dramatically, gesturing to her, the balcony, the night, in some furious soliloquy.

She was staggering backwards. She had seen this face before. Felt this grip. She knew. And so, she should be crying out. Didn't know why she couldn't. Just staggering backwards while he clenched her wrists together; his large hands now encompassed hers and wrapped her left wrist over her right. She was pinned, entangled – and she pictured chickens strung up in the market, ham hocks on chains and hooks.

"Let me – please, Daniel. Just let me go."

She was squirming, pathetic, hopeless but not hurt yet. She was not hurt yet. She would fight, this time. This time she would fight.

She tried to stamp one foot onto his, and missed, feeling the tendons of her ankle pop — snap- as she jarred against the tiles. She gave a yelp. He shook his head, moving his face, his body closer. Then she was flicking her forehead back and forth, a broken puppet, trying to headbutt him. Missing, slipping, nodding, inept, as she edged further backwards with robotic baby steps until she was up against the low, tiled wall of the balcony.

He smirked.

She tried for one last time to make contact, but he broke free from her, easily, smoothly, stepping to the side, laughing as she fell forwards, her temple hitting the tiles. Her lips kissing the floor. Only one arm broke her fall this time — the other concertinaed and crumpled under her body.

"Jesus," he said. "What a joke."

She stayed still for a moment, iron-tongued, sticky-mawed, vaguely aware that her forehead was pressing onto the floor. That her arm felt dull and hot. Her mouth was swollen and full.

Perhaps she should pretend to pass out. If she did it now, he might stop.

But she felt both his arms wrap around her waist, his fingers locked together in a cat's cradle at the front, pulling in and up on her abdomen in a sordid Heimlich manoeuvre. Yanking her backwards, up, by her stomach. She saw a string of pink falling from her face towards the floor, falling in a waterfall of bile and blood. Was she being sick? She wasn't sure.

On the floor, she could see an extraordinary pattern of dark red blood — dots where her knees had been, a string where her mouth was, almost joining the splatter of her forehead. It was stunning and sharp against the tiles; the evening light turned it almost black. Like a pattern of leaves. Or a murder of crows.

She tried to find herself in space, to navigate the air, twirling her one good arm around her and searching for the floor as he puppeted her about, toes dragging, skimming, but not finding ballast.

"Wha—" She tried but could not. She could not.

"Keep still and I'll let you go. Just keep—"

She did what he said.

He kept his arms around her but let her drop to the ground so that her feet were in place, and she rested back against him. This should be a tender embrace. Might seem it, from afar, through someone else's eyes. Would have been, once. But that was long ago, now. Long gone.

"You've marked your face, you stupid bitch. You'll have marks on your face, now." He was muttering to himself.

They stood for a moment, and she kept herself as still as she could. Then he let go of her torso, one arm away from her body so that she thought she would hit the floor again, but he grabbed her hair to stop her.

"Look at what you've done!"

"…I'm sorry," she managed.

By her hair, he directed her over towards the wall of the balcony.

"Stand there," he said. "If you're capable."

She felt the back of her heels against the cool surface, the feeling creeping up her legs, her hips, as she pushed against the short wall to steady herself. She was at the edge. He stepped forward until his face was next to hers, pupils tracing across her, trained in on her forehead, then her nose, her mouth and lips bruised and squashed like a ripe pear.

176

"Well, that's attractive," he said, leering. "Come on then, let's see the rest of you. Let's see the damage."

He grabbed the bottom of her dress and yanked upwards, greedily, rough, a child with Christmas paper. Ineffectually, she tried to push him away.

"No."

He lifted her dress up to her chin and pinned it in place with his left forearm. Exposing her, smiling at the dappled greys and greens across her torso, tenderly touching a faded thumbprint above her hip, the old bruise almost gone.

She leant back, her body arching steeply over the edge, away from him, as far away as she could. She was propped on the edge of the balcony. He dropped her dress and pulled at his flies, trying to rip buttons from their holes, rushing, frantic.

"No, Daniel, I don't—"

He swung the back of his hand across her face, sending a splatter through the air.

"Shut the fuck up."

He turned his attention back to removing his jeans.

The vision in her right eye clouded over with cotton-wool white. She leant forward and wretched, vomiting, real vomit this time, with stench and texture.

He stopped. Looked to the ground, eyes, and mouth twitching. Slowly, he lifted his head up towards her face. She looked at him through her blonde hair, pebble-dashed with detritus.

He raised both arms to her shoulders, and with one swift, effortless movement, he shoved her, hard.

And then she fell.

177

Chapter 20

For many years now, I had been growing lilies; you always remarked upon them when you came to the flat. I had white and pink Asiatics in tubs and didn't deserve the lovely bloom they gave each year as I did so little to tend to them. They were well-established and apparently self-sufficient. Before that, I had tiger lilies. And I had tried and failed to grow arum lilies in the bed in the corner of the patio – it was probably too dry, yet I loved their architectural, regal form so had attempted more than once.

When you were very young, perhaps six, or seven, you said you wanted to change your name to Daisy: remember? For several weeks, when the mood took you, and you remembered, you would even insist on being called by Daisy, and refused to answer to Susie. Jack then took to calling you 'Daisy Chain the Pain,' singing an off-tune little song he had devised, and after a while, it lost its attraction. Nonetheless, you continued to be entranced by plants for years, moving on from a desire to be renamed, to musings of what you might call your own daughter when you had her – which seemed a certainty back then. Jonquil. Flora. Heather.

It wasn't only the beauty of flowers that appealed to you, you were also fascinated by their resilience, and complexity. You read books on wildlife and conservation, and before the divorce, in the old house, you had your own plot in the garden where you sowed wildflowers and daffodil bulbs while you wore your ubiquitous red wellies. You tracked their progress on charts stuck to the fridge, and you labelled them with care on little wooden sticks.

For a while, I wondered if you would be a botanist, a horticulturist, a conservationist – and you always did remain green-fingered. You never lost your interest in the science of plants, commenting on soil acidity and the role of creepy crawlies in a way that was foreign to me. I was a keen gardener, but too impatient to research. I just liked the pretty bits: the colours, the birds.

At this time of year, the lilies died back, and my beds were transformed into spikes and blooms of violet and blue as little asters and giant agapanthus took over the patio borders and the remaining pots of the patio. You would have told me off for not moving the latter into the sun, or even bringing the pot inside. I have always been a lazier gardener than you were.

I cut myself a small bunch of blue for the kitchen table and went back inside to drink some tea and have some lunch.

I turned on the television for the lunchtime news, my sandwich balanced on a cushion on my lap and tea within easy reach, feeling cosy and peaceful. I had just taken a large bite – tomato seeds falling back to the plate like tapioca – when the third or fourth story was about a holiday accident. And a balcony.

I stopped, and stared at the screen, aware of the masticated bread coagulating into a lump in my mouth. A 24-year-old British male had fallen from a balcony in Majorca. The police thought he was 'balconing' – an all too familiar phrase to me, which I had learnt, quickly, to despise. Jumping from one balcony to another for fun, or from a balcony into a pool. It was a phrase filled with judgement.

The people who had suggested this didn't know you. You weren't anything like the victims who did these things. Believe me, I know how that sounds; how I sound. I know I risk being called a snob, or in denial. I don't like hearing myself this way. But honestly, I don't mean you were different by class, finances, or education. I mean in personality. In your spirit. They seemed to be vivacious party people, most of them. The life and soul. Living in the moment. Loved by all. Yet it would be unspeakably out of character to you to act the daredevil, or the fool, or to be so spontaneous. You were a reserved, quiet spirit, always. You were not the type of riotous larger-than-life prankster depicted in these stories.

Though perhaps this mother thought the same. Her child was different, too.

Nobody wants their loved ones to be reduced to a stereotype.

He was alive, the young man – thank God – but in a serious condition. It was the second day of his holiday with a group of male friends. It was suspected that he had tried to hop from his balcony to an adjoining one where some of his mates were. An image was displayed of the ugly, multi-storey hotel on the screen. The balconies looked to be almost touching; the risk not too great to the young and inebriated, I considered.

He suffered head injuries, but they hoped there would be no long-term effects from these, a statement from his mother said. He had a compound fracture in one leg, three broken ribs and a punctured lung. He also had no travel insurance, and now his mother – pictured fleetingly, raw, charging through a stream of journalists and photographers - had set up a fundraising page for him.

I turned off the television, put my plate down on the table, and for a moment I stared at the blank screen. I was at risk here. At risk of being overwhelmed, carried away, drowning. The unexpected story had thrown me straight in, and I felt the old sensation of dropping underneath, then up and under, gagging, gasping, not quite above the surface, not quite safe and secure. I did not want this. Didn't want the unhappy, bloodied memories of you to overwhelm the happy ones. Didn't want uncontrollable tears, headachy hours of talking to myself about the injustice, praying that it was not true. None of it was true. I was tired of this.

I lay down, pulling the blanket from the back of the sofa around me.

***

The room was dim when I was awoken by the ringtone of my mobile phone. I felt woozy and dry, confused. It took me a moment to understand the

181

source of the noise, and then to locate the phone. It was Jack.

"Hi, mumster," he said, warmly.

"Hi, sweetheart. Give me a moment?"

I leaned over to the lamp and switched it on, illuminating the curling sandwich and undrunk cup of tea from earlier.

"What time is it?" I asked, yawning.

"Had an old lady sleep, have you? Bless."

"Very funny. I can assure you I don't make a habit of it. I must have needed it." Though it was the second time it had happened in the last few weeks, so perhaps that was no longer true.

The sleep had been deep and unpleasant; images were still in my mind, confused: of young men cycling bicycles off the edge of cliffs; young girls jumping from ridiculously high diving boards; of myself crawling along, legs useless, crawling, skinned and broken, at a painstaking pace up a steep, craggy hill.

"Well, how are you?" Jack asked.

"I can't even think straight yet. You talk. Talk to me. Tell me what you've been up to."

He chattered away for fifteen minutes about his garden and a night out at a new pub, which had opened within walking distance of their home, set in an old Post Office building.

"Finally! Somewhere decent that doesn't involve taxis or a half an hour bus journey each way."

"I think that's a good reason for me to pencil in a trip to see you," I said. "I was thinking of coming up and tying it in with Christmas shopping, early

December? We could even make it our fake Christmas, seeing as you're abandoning your darling mother until New Year."

"You know I have to work. Can't let the biddies down."

"But you're happy to desert this one?" I laughed.

"When you can't manage your roasties anymore and I am spoon-feeding you mash, that's when I'll make sure to come for Christmas."

"You are shockingly irreverent! I hope your bosses don't ever get to hear you talk like this. And as if you'd stoop so low as to feed people these days. Don't you have staff for that?"

"You know full well I don't mean it. And yes, actually, I regularly feed the clients. I love all the old ladies in my life... Well, yes. Anyway... early December would be wonderful. Text me possible dates and I'll work magic to ensure we are both free."

"Great," I said. "I'll look forward to it." And I would.

"O.K. then, best go. So... everything is alright then? You're... alright?"

He, too, had seen the news and was checking up on me.

"Oh, yes. I'll be fine," I said. "Bye, sweetheart."

I disconnected the mobile and sat for a moment curled up in my blanket, rubbing my eyes to get rid of the last dregs of dreams and drowsiness. The sensor light in the patio flicked on, as it did sometimes, Toby's cat from next door taking a shortcut usually.

I stood slowly, stretching, even making a half-hearted attempt to bend down towards my knees to loosen up my back. I got to the patio doors and pulled the sheer curtains apart, for a moment wondering if I might see a crow, or a bloodstain on the glass; but no, I was foolish to think so. I would not let this memory set in. There was no one there, and no animal in sight.

I was about to turn back and go to make some coffee when I realised that some of the plants looked different. I stopped in my tracks; felt my chest tighten. It took me a second to process what I saw: bent down towards the slabs and the borders, stalks snapped, flowers compressed, were the blooms of my blue asters.

Chapter 21

I was washing the kitchen floor when my landline rang. This was unusual these days – and it filled me with a feeling of dread. The last time it had been Tim, to tell me of Rose's death. What now? I raced to the phone in the hallway, walking my bare feet across the newly mopped tiles.

"Hello?" I was out of breath.

"Good morning, could I speak to Mrs Bevan, please?"

Bevan: your father's name. I hadn't heard that in a while.

"There's no Mrs Bevan here," I said, irritated. "There's a Catherine Keely. Is that who you mean?"

"Mother of Susie Bevan?"

"Susie Bevan-Keely. Look, sorry… who is this?"

"Apologies, Mrs Keely, I just—"

"Ms."

"Sorry?"

"I am Ms Catherine Keely," I said slowly, through gritted teeth.

A faint laugh dripped into his voice, raising my hackles still further.

"Ms. Keely… My name is David Jones. I'm a freelance journalist – a broadsheet journalist. I don't suppose you have a minute to talk?"

He sounded plummy, sycophantic, late middle-aged. He had a hint of a Welsh accent.

"About what?"

I could feel a tremor rising up from my chest, through my neck, and cheeks. Anxiety. Emotion. And anger.

"I wonder if you've heard the terribly sad news about the young man who has suffered injuries in Majorca. He fell from a balcony. I am compiling an in-depth piece on the prevalence of these accidents, why they happen and the trauma the families are put through. I know your daughter…" I heard him flipping pages in a notebook, "Susie, she passed away under similar circumstances?"

"Is that a question? Because the answer is no."

"Sorry?" He was perplexed. "'No' to speaking to me?"

"No," I said. "No, she did not pass away under similar circumstances."

"Oh, but I understood she did fall from a balcony, in Crete, wasn't it?"

"That doesn't make it the same."

"Well, no. It wasn't the same location, but –"

"If someone had a car crash because the other driver fell asleep at the wheel and drove into them, is that the same as crashing your own car because you were drunk? If someone trips, is that the same as fainting? If someone got knocked over in the road, would that be the same as death by suicide, jumping out in front of a car? If someone slips and falls, is that the same as doing bloody long jump?"

"I'm not sure I follow –"

"I am saying, Mr Jones, that just because a balcony is involved, that doesn't make every incident the same. They are all individual cases. Individual bloody people, for that matter."

"Right. O.K. perhaps not… but if you'd be willing to chat to me, perhaps meet me, you could explain to me the difference?" he said. "Tell me why your daughter's story was different?"

"Wait, though, hang on." I jumped in again. "I'm not saying she's the only one that's different. I said they are each different." I heard his breath rustle down the line in heavy blows. "And I don't think her accident being different makes her better. Or me better, somehow. I don't want my daughter treated with respect and everyone else's treated like dirt. They all need respect. They are kids." I slammed a hand against the wall. "Victims. Just because someone has a brief moment of recklessness, does that mean they deserve to die? I am getting sick of seeing people being vilified. I want bloody accuracy, that's all… is that too much to ask? If it needs reporting at all, that is."

There was an uncomfortably long silence. I was shaking. I had no idea how he would react.

"O.K…" He started. "If you could give me some times when you are free to meet, we could talk all this through."

"Why though? Why would I?"

"Well, to contribute to the article. Accurately."

There was a patronising edge to his voice that grated on me.

"But what exactly is your article about?"

"I thought I had said, Catherine… Can I call you Catherine?"

"No."

"Apologies. Again. Anyway… it's a human-interest story. It won't be… vilifying anyone. It's about the people behind the photos."

"Yes, but what is the focus? The angle? Accidents on holiday? Or young people taking risks? Alcohol? Unexplained deaths? Wasted lives?"

I could hear my voice getting even louder, higher, my resentment breaking through the tremor. I told myself not to cry. Do not cry. You are doing a good job. You are. Don't give him an excuse to dismiss you.

"Ms Keely… essentially, I'm writing about the tragedy; the human angle; the families left behind," he said.

"That sounds very virtuous, Mr Jones. And yet here you are cold calling a grieving mother to get your paycheck. Will you be putting that in your article? The random phone calls we get. And how did you get this number, anyway?"

I was furious now, struggling to keep my composure.

"I… Is it ex-directory? Oh, I'm sorry, I assumed there wasn't an issue. I was given it readily by one of your daughter's friends. I got the impression you would welcome the call – would want to give your point of view, to put the record straight. I am sure that readers would find you very compelling. You seem to have a lot to… a strong voice. But… perhaps I was wrong?"

"Daniel," I stated.

"Pardon?"

"Daniel gave you my number."

"I don't want to go into conversations I have had with other parties, Ms Keely. You'll understand that. Look, I do feel that we have gotten off on the wrong foot here. I really do want to explore this sensitively. From what I've found, these resorts have got off scot-free… The responsibility of the hotels – they promote their resorts as party places for young people and they are more than happy to take their money. They offer discount drinks. Then they inadequately protect them. They definitely have a part to play in reducing balconing incidents. They also have to—"

"What did you say?"

"I said they have a responsibility, too. They need to look at their happy hour prices, the railing heights. Balconing wouldn't be happening if—"

"Balconing?" I asked, quietly.

"Yes—"

I put the phone down.

***

I had to get out after that. I grabbed the nearest shoes I could find and slipped them onto my damp feet – picked up my wallet and keys and went out. Walking down the road I had the familiar irritation of realising I had no pockets, then chose to put one object in each hand, swinging my arms like pendulums, feeling armed and irate, with my

Birkenstocks and bare ankles. I headed towards the shop, unsure where else to go. I hadn't been going there on a whim lately, having overspent in the last couple of months with meals out, the gala, and the funeral trip.

I couldn't believe Daniel would give a journalist my number. I wondered what he had told him; I wondered if he was being paid. I should have tried to establish what paper the journalist would be hawking this story to, so that I could read it on publication – if he ever sold it, that is. I wondered if I should call him back myself, give him a grilling, and put him on the spot for once. I imagined myself penning my own article about the anguish of being bullied and mistreated by the press. But then, who would ever publish that?

I was weighing up whether to call Daniel and give him an earful or to be more gracious and restrained. It didn't come easy to me to contain myself when I was upset – although I had gotten better as I got older. The only times Tim and I had ever fought were when I had exploded in fury on suspicion of something I felt he had done intentionally to spite or hurt me – forgotten your parents' evening and made other plans (twice) or gone out until the early hours the night before a Christening, for example. It took me years to realise that most men are not that cynical and premeditated. They don't plan to do things to hurt you; they just do what they feel like at the time. They aren't always good at anticipating consequences, in my experience. Yes, I know. I shouldn't generalise.

Perhaps that was what had happened with Daniel. Perhaps he hadn't thought through the impact of passing on my number. Or maybe he didn't even chat to Mr Jones and simply tried to pass him on to me. Just to get him off his back, make his life easier for that brief moment. That did seem feasible.

Whatever had happened, I wished he had given me some warning.

By the time I reached the shop, I felt sadder, more resigned, and let down, than I did angry - and I was no longer craving banana loaf or chocolate. Instead, I bought a newspaper and a carton of juice. I even resisted the seedlings at the front door.

I walked back at a more leisurely pace, considering how odd it was to be the subject of media attention, and how cruel the world is that such stories exist for entertainment.

***

Sat with my orange juice at the kitchen table, I flicked through the paper, wondering if I would see an attribution to David Jones, or a story on the Majorcan accident. I was cross with myself that I had not paid attention to the young man's name. He deserved better. But I found nothing on him at all – and I was both sad and relieved that he was already yesterday's news.

I was compelled to find my file of newspaper clippings; I didn't know if this was a healthy response or not, but it was better than firing off a text at Daniel. Anything was. I had to think for a moment to locate it; there was a time when it was a permanent fixture in the kitchen or near the sofa, but I had put it away around six months ago, under the bed, next to a suitcase of some of your clothes. Eventually, those clothes would make it to a charity shop, I imagined, and the cuttings would end up in the bin. But not yet.

The file started with clippings about you, of course. Local, and a couple of national newspaper articles, circled and annotated where they had got facts wrong, so many times. Lazy; insulting. Your name. Your age. Where you were from. One of them had even described you as a 'teacher and part-time model.' It was as if only beautiful girls deserved to be grieved over. Or perhaps trying to elicit some lust in their readers, over the hot, dead girl. Either way, the motivation for this blatant lie was grotesque.

In some of the articles they quoted Alexander, the manager of the hotel: he was deeply sorry the accident had happened, but he assured everyone that such incidents were rare, and there were no suspicious circumstances. The same phraseology appeared several times, and at the time I had wondered if he had been provided with a quote from a lawyer, or the complex owners, perhaps. On reflection, it occurred to me now, that perhaps he had only ever been interviewed once, and all these various journalists had appropriated and re-used the same lines from him, over and over, until even he had no voice.

After a while, the articles were mixed in with those about other incidents: balcony falls onto rooftops diving into pools, dropping onto dining areas, pathways. They were mostly young people, often male – pictured smiling, sunburnt or tanned in the photos that accompanied the articles – although there were a couple of incidents involving older men on holiday with their family, or young women, or children. There was one heart-breaking story about a seven-year-old boy, and I flicked over that page, knowing when to expect it, having seen it so many times.

Not all of the victims had died. Several had survived and recovered, one had lost his hand and forearm, and another, a young woman, had been paralysed but appeared to be making progress. I ran my finger over her face in the picture, smiling at the camera from her hospital bed, her exhausted mother looking down on her. Her right cheek was laced with a web of scars. But I was glad for them. You would be, too.

I had thought about setting up a support group when I started collecting these tales. I remembered discussing it with Jayne, and I even mentioned it to Tim. Jayne thought it a great idea, channelling my frenetic energy into something concrete and positive. Of course, she would. Tim was less sure, thought it might lead to me wallowing and obsessing. It never came to fruition as I never reached a point where I felt I could be a support for anyone. I was worried that other members might look to me for answers, if I did it, when I was still awash with questions. How could it be that I still was, all this time later?

Chapter 22

I received a friend request from Jackson Smith's mother. He was the young man who was recovering in Majorca. Jackson. I had been playing around on my phone, passing the time as it was a damp day and I had achieved lots of housework that morning. I couldn't afford online shopping and it was too early for dinner. Social media was the obvious – unimaginative – choice.

Jackson's mother was called Sandra. I looked at her profile and found several recent posts with public security settings. Presumably, this was for ease of sharing to help with publicising their story, as scrolling down her profile showed me that earlier posts and pictures had been private.

Her cover picture was a photo of a smiling Jackson looking straight at the camera, while she leant back to gaze up at him, in adoration. She looked around the same age as me, or perhaps slightly older. She had blonde hair, cut mid-length, and was wearing a cotton dress in the picture; unfashionable and practical, but bright, cheerful pink.

In stark contrast, her profile picture was a photo of him in hospital, on a drip: bruised, squashed, distorted, unconscious. Static. The photograph was embellished with the motto 'Bring Jackson Home.'

I felt I was intruding on her personal grief, even though she had placed this in the public domain. It was so personal, so very human, this picture. Intimate. I was nauseous to see his face, his fragility. I felt exposed, and that she was, too. Perhaps there was reasoning behind this. The shock factor. The pull. Or perhaps she was simply absorbed in grief.

Her most recent post explained that he was making slow progress and that they had set an initial fundraising target of £20,000 towards the cost of bringing him home by air ambulance, once he was stable enough. Almost 200 comments beneath expressed sorrow, hope and love. She had replied to one, saying, "I've got some ideas for promoting the fundraising. Newspapers on my side. We will smash this target and more for Jack. Watch this space!"

Her use of the diminutive 'Jack' made my stomach heave, my own boy, my own Jack came into view, and I shut the page and put my phone down for a while, taking a glass of water onto the patio to steady myself in the misty autumn air. I sat outside and filled my lungs with the damp atmosphere, washing from the inside out. I tried not to look over to the stumps in the flower bed. This was too much. I could only deal with one drama at a time.

I suspected that she was getting in touch with me, to help her with her appeal somehow. And she had mentioned newspapers, campaigning, essentially. That filled me with alarm.

It occurred to me that perhaps, in fact, it was she who had orchestrated the article with David Jones. Perhaps she had piqued his interest; given him the idea. Maybe she had even suggested that he hunt me down.

Hunted. That was how I felt. When I wanted to be left alone.

What would you have done, in my place? I already knew the answer, I think. But you were a kinder person than I am, and stronger in several ways.

I walked back indoors; my skin pricked by the chill air. I found myself wandering around the flat, uneasy, restless.

Besides, I was busy; it was approaching Christmas now and I had events; a trip to South Wales; Christmas shopping; Daniel's party. And a lot on my mind. Too many things going wrong. Accidents. Coincidences. A stalker. There. I had admitted it. There was a good chance I was being stalked. It seemed ridiculous. Incredible. Unreal.

I would be of no help to her, Sandra Smith. I could not commit enough time to do her child justice.

I found myself sitting on the edge of my bed, staring at a photograph of you in graduation cap and gown – staring until these brittle truths, or half-truths, perhaps, disintegrated around me.

I knew I would have to accept her request.

***

I waited until the next day before I acted. After morning coffee, I clicked to accept and then sent her a one-sentence message to say that I was sorry to hear of her son's accident. I put the phone down and applied a hair treatment, then had a shower. I didn't pick up the phone again until after I had dressed and blow-dried my hair. It took significant restraint not to keep checking, yet there was nothing from Sandra Smith when I finally came back to the phone.

I reflected and then felt ridiculous to have imagined she would be so quick to respond to me when she must have been immersed in arrangements, communication with her family, and worry. It was arrogant to have thought I would be top of her list.

From the fridge, I retrieved a couple of leeks that had seen better days, and started chopping to make soup for lunch, later. I turned on the radio and my mind drifted to you, as it so often did, remembering how I had shown you how to make lentil soup (your favourite), and casserole with dumplings (Jack's). You were not a fussy eater, and you enjoyed the smells, colours, and textures of food. Or at least, you did when you were younger. The kitchen in the old house had been huge, with a wooden island in the middle, where you would sit precariously on your knees on a high stool and lean in, observing as I sliced and diced. We were lucky. You persuaded me to let you join in with the preparation from a surprisingly young age – but you never cut yourself. You were always very dexterous. And cautious, too.

My phone pinged and I took the pan off the heat. But it was a text from Jessica asking if she could pop around, later. I messaged back, gladly, that I was free all evening and suggested seven o'clock.

It was later in the afternoon when I heard from Sandra. I went for a short walk to get some air, minus my phone, and when I came home found that she had replied to my message, thanking me for accepting her request. She had spent some time seeking other mothers whose children had fallen from balconies and came across your story. How easy it is to find people in this day and age. I am nobody of interest, yet she tracked me down in days.

We sent a few short messages back and forth until I asked her what her plans were for raising the profile of her fundraising: *You mentioned the papers? In my experience they are fickle, but hopefully their involvement works out for you.*

I wanted to give some advice, without overstepping my mark. But I also didn't want her to think I was an expert ear, or someone solid to lean on. I was neither of those things. In all honesty, I was also angling, trying to move things along so that I could hear whether there was some specific reason for her contacting me. Was she involved with that Jones man, the journalist? Was she going to ask me to put my face to her fundraising, or join some sort of group of aggrieved or grieving mums, perhaps? Of course, I wasn't famous. But your picture had been featured in several papers, and a blonde, attractive young woman was a good addition to any publicity. Cynical, I know.

Oh, just the local rag. I have a friend who is a sportswriter there. He is doing a sponsored head shave for me. Should get us a grand or two, I hope.

I felt sorry and sad that this was the extent of the exposure she could get for her child, and confused, still, as to why she had gotten in touch. I was still waiting for the big reveal.

Sorry, have to go now, Cath. I hope you don't think it is weird that I got in touch with you. There are lots of people here giving me sympathy and support, but they don't understand because they can't, but I thought you might. Thank you for chatting with me x x It helps x

Guilty, crushed at the bare simplicity of her explanation, my hands shook as I replied: *Any time, day, or night. Let me know if I can help you, somehow. X*

***

"So, she just wanted to chat, then?" said Jessica.

"Yes, just a few messages. She said she wanted to touch base with someone who would understand how she felt. I felt odd about it at first. But to be honest, it was nice in the end."

Jessica didn't reply.

"Are you O.K.?" I asked.

"Yeah… sorry. It's just, for some reason I got excited and thought you were going to say that there was some bizarre connection to Susie's accident."

"I… Oh! Well, it's not even the same country, so… What do you mean?'"

"I don't know. That the same company owned the hotels, or the same designer decided the balcony height, maybe. I never trusted that bloke who managed the place. The one with the hair gel," she octopused her fingers over her head to indicate his hair, and I smiled. "It crossed my mind you were going to say he worked there now or something."

"Ah, I see. Well, not that I am aware of. And Alexander still works in Crete. I saw him."

"Really? Wow. I'm clutching at straws, I guess," she said.

"I know that feeling," I muttered. "Anyway, I was almost about to start accusing her of getting in touch so she could use me in some media campaign. I saw some comments that she had posted about getting the press involved – you know how much I love the papers. But it turned out to be something local. Nothing to do with me at all. It was embarrassing, really, the realisation that I had managed to twist her story to rotate around me. When it's nothing to do with me. And she hadn't given me much thought. But I haven't had a great week, thanks to Daniel, and I rather got myself in a paranoid muddle."

"Daniel?" she asked. "Oh, while I think of it, he's the reason I asked to pop around. He's invited me to his birthday, and I gather you're on the guest list, too. I can't decide whether I can face it. Are you going?"

"God, no. Can you believe he put some nasty little freelancer onto me for a story about Susie? He even gave him my home phone number."

There was a pause. She looked at the worktop.

"That's the reason you're not going?"

"Isn't that enough?" I asked, bemused.

"Well, no. Look, sorry to say this but I think you're going to need to dig out your party dress after all. Because it wasn't Daniel who gave Mr Jones your name and number. It was me."

"What? What do you mean?"

I was in the middle of ripping open the paper of a herbal tea bag. I stopped, hands aloft, the edge of the packet curling around my forefinger.

"God, look... I'm... I'm desperately sorry, I am. He sort of... tricked me. I was stupid. It was an accident. I feel like a right—"

"But how?"

I dropped my hands to the worktop. My head was swimming. I was thrown. Was she covering up for Daniel? No. Why would she?

"Right. Give me a minute. I'll rewind."

She put both hands down on the surface, the tips of her fingers touching mine. I waited for a beat, and then shuffled them away. I needed to hear what she said, first.

"So... he called me and told me about that Jackson boy. I hadn't heard and it was... it was awful. Well, you know what it's like when you hear something like that. You of all people must know. So, I was shaking – literally shaking – and he was there telling me everything in minute detail about the fall. And the aftermath. I was transfixed and sort of horrified, but I didn't cut him off – I don't know why. I was just there, listening to him share all those awful, traumatic details about that poor boy in the deep, calm voice of his until all of a sudden he even started to list his injuries. Matter of fact. This catalogue of trauma and bleeding and breaking and I realised I needed to stop him."

I pictured Jackson; the image shared on social media. Wires, bruises, swelling.

"No, that I actually could stop him, and I didn't have to listen. So, I thought, and I tried to cut him off. I think I swore or something. And I was going to cut him off, phone down, when he said your name and it made me pause. He said he had your number and wanted to speak to you. He said he was calling everyone connected with Susie; her mother was a key figure, of course. And it would be better to get your thoughts directly, rather than guessing them. And that's true, right?"

"I... well, not exactly. I mean, why did he need to write about my thoughts at all?"

My voice was flat. This still didn't make sense.

"Ok, I know that, now. I know none of it was true. I'm so bloody stupid. I'm so angry with myself. But when he said he had your number but thought he had written it down incorrectly – he asked me to pass on the landline number, to be sure – I... I... just did. For some reason, I imagined that you were already expecting his call. But of course, it was a lie. Of course, he was..."

"Lying." I finished for her.

"Yes," she said, quietly.

I made the tea automatically. It was in a china cup, too hot to drink or touch. I passed her the tea, and she cupped it between both hands, and it crossed my mind that it would be extremely hot, the cup, and might scald her. Briefly, this thought made me happy. Next came shame.

She carried on, wittering an apology. She felt ridiculous that evening when it struck her how obvious this was, she told me. And she had crossed her fingers in the hope that for some reason he would never get in touch with me, and I wouldn't have to know anything about it.

Really, it wasn't her foolishness, the accidental betrayal that upset me so much. It was the humiliation of being shown, again, how easily – happily, even – I came to extreme conclusions about Daniel. It was my own behaviour that troubled me the most. It was not pleasant to have irrefutable evidence of my flawed judgement when it came to him, and how deeply I was prejudiced against him.

He hadn't given David Jones – that damn journalist – my number. And I had never had any evidence or reason to think he had even spoken to him.

Jessica was generally a sharp and cynical person, impervious to deceit. The first to call someone out. It seemed out of character. And yet, then I had a flash of a memory of her calling me, drunk, emotional - and it struck me she was still grieving, this girl. Still mourning her friend. And young. And we could all be forgiven for having poor judgement during weak moments. I didn't want to think too harshly of her. I pictured her juddering, agitated on the phone with this smooth and confident man. It was odd, but not impossible to see how he could have fooled her.

Chapter 24

We had agreed that we would accompany each other to the party; me, out of guilt, and Jessica from some perverse curiosity and fear of missing out, I guessed. I had told her I would text to confirm by the 10th of November. That had been and gone, and within a day or two she would be chasing me up on it.

Daniel was turning thirty. Something you never would. I recalled his birthday two years ago – or was it three? When you had come to mine, having asked for help in baking him a cake. I am not a great baker, so I was an odd sort of support to you. We stood together in the small kitchen of my flat, fumbling and flitting between snapping at each other and giggling, while trying to navigate a complex recipe, which called for a fluted cake tin and folding things together in a bowl. I remembered laughing as you realised you had forgotten to add the flour at the correct moment: you spun around in a panic and sprayed an angel wing of powder through the air, which then danced across the floor. Your bare feet were talcumed in dust by the end. Patterns laced the tiles like animal prints where you had pottered back and forth from one surface to another.

You brought me a chunk of cake two days later and it tasted passably good. I briefly considered trying to find the recipe again and then recreate it for his party, this year. Then I realised this might be considered an odd thing to do. Macabre, even.

I decided to commit to this party, and to order him some sort of present. I found my laptop and sat on the sofa, looking for personalised gifts. Typing in 'gifts for men' and 'men's gifts, 30th birthday' to find something appropriate, inoffensive, and bland. Personal and yet generic; it was not an easy task. Daniel leaned towards the upmarket and stylish, and my frame of reference for him was linked to his relationship with you.

I spent well over an hour, flicking between pages and adding random shiny things to my 'basket,' until a light in the garden caught my eye. For a brief moment, I felt anxious. I still did not like to think of all the things that had happened. Refused to let this fear consume me, so I didn't allow the feeling to settle in, I steeled myself and looked up to see Toby's cat frozen in the beam, in the middle of the patio. My curtains were open and the room in the half-light; I hadn't realised the time. It was fading into evening, already.

I stood up and went to the double door to pull the sheer curtains tight, glancing out to see the first stars kissing the clouded, autumn sky. I paused for a moment, enjoying the peace. Then, I turned the lamp on and went back to the laptop, realising with a jolt that I had strayed off course and had been browsing through birthday gifts for 30-year-old-women. That was when I stopped.

I picked up my phone and texted Jessica: *I'm going to the party. Will be getting Daniel a voucher, probably to*

The Lexington Hotel? He can have dinner or stay over. Seems his sort of place (?). Let me know if you want to come in on it and if so, how much. Speak soon. x

She tried to shut the door, but they were still intertwined, and he had a flip-flopped foot, a hand, an elbow in the way. They laughed into each other's faces. She could see the bridge of his nose, the filaments of bristle on his upper lip. There was the sour tang of lager as he leaned in, to kiss her again.

She pushed against the door edge; he squeezed out of the way, shuffling himself around without extricating himself from the embrace.

"You big softie," she said and giggled.

She leapt away from him, taking two steps further into the hotel room as she turned, twisting in a fractured pirouette, dancing for him, playfully, coquettishly.

Her bare feet skidded on the tiles as she raced towards the balcony.

"I want to see the view!" she cried.

He groaned.

"I just want a shower," he said. "I feel greasy and tired."

"Ate too much, you mean."

"There's no such thing."

The bathroom door gaped then crashed against the wall; she heard it, didn't look back – as she yanked the sliding doors open, enough to squeeze through. She stepped into the warmth of the night. The breeze lifted the scent of mint and chlorine up towards her.

She leant forward to try to see the view between the rooftops. She felt her shins against the cool surface, the feeling creeping up her legs, her hips, as she pushed further against the short wall. She was at the edge of the balcony. In the distance, she could hear low singing through the water of a shower. Tuneless, but lovely.

As she stood, face in the wind, she caught a familiar figure from the corner of her eye. He had come out onto his balcony in the next block and then gone in again. Wet trunks now hung and dripped from the broken drying rail.

She called out to him. Of course, she knew it was futile; she was nervous to shout too loudly; it was late, and children were in bed. He would never have heard her.

The apartments were built into ugly, irregular shapes with different floors projecting out to varying degrees. The blocks tessellated together into a jigsaw, so that her balcony overhung theirs, by a few inches, even though she was in B, and they were in A.

She considered throwing something down – a paper aeroplane or a random funny object, for her own amusement. The rubber duck from the bathroom, perhaps. But that would mean interrupting him and his vocal acrobatics.

She leant further forwards, her body arching steeply over the edge, as far as she could, while holding the top of the balcony.

An exciting, peculiar idea sparked in her. She felt it flickering.

She had always played things quite safe. But this holiday, the sun, the beach, her friends - it had lifted her up out of herself, somehow. She had started to feel there could be more, beyond the confines of this role she had carved for herself. Or perhaps it was the role that everyone else had carved for her. Either way, she was a little too young and imaginative for this pigeon-hole she'd been placed into.

It couldn't be that hard.

She was light, fit, and nimble. She had always been dexterous and agile.

There was one plastic chair on the balcony, and she brought it over to where she had been standing, angling it carefully to align it with the position she would need to be in, to clamber *safely over and down. She needed to be sure that she could reach the other balcony without jumping far. She only needed to drop down, or jump half a metre or so, no more. It seemed feasible. She would go over to the ledge on the other side of the balcony and then clamber down. Like a climbing frame. Like a playground*

She placed the chair carefully and then stepped back to survey the scene, leaning over again to see below. This was a domino run, or a snooker game. It needed to be accurate, with angles just so.

Stepping up onto the white chair, she felt the plastic legs buckle, then settle. She held the edge of the balcony with both hands and then, with surprising ease, she lifted her legs up and spun them over the top, still holding on — one after the other. The balcony edge was low, even for someone as small as she was. She balanced her feet on the small shelf that protruded on the other side, and cried out, exhilarated. She couldn't believe what she had done. She was already halfway there.

This ledge was narrower than she had realised but her feet were small. She looked down, cautiously, and noticed that she had misjudged where to climb over. She needed to be further along. And perhaps the next block was further away than she realised, not quite overlapping hers. Not quite. Or was it? It was hard to see from here. The light was dim. And it was hard to look down without a swell of anxiety rising within.

She crab-walked her way along the ledge to get herself closer to where she needed to be. She moved delicately, all the while thinking that she would stop in a moment and climb back over. Surely, she would. This had been a ridiculous idea. Yet something in her kept her going. Recklessness? Excitement? Stubbornness? She wasn't sure.

Perhaps she was tipsier than she had realised.

210

But she was almost there. How they would laugh, in shock and admiration when she arrived. How amazed everyone would be.

Then she felt the toes on her right foot touch something damp as she skimmed it further along – and without warning her foot was slipping, sliding off the narrow surface, then her right hand broke free from the balcony as her body jerked down to follow her foot. Her left hand was trying but failing to hold her weight; it unlocked from the balcony: both hands then briefly lacing in the air as her fingers touched the balcony once, twice, but never quite reached it.

She cried out. Cartwheeled her arms.

And then she fell.

Chapter 25

I couldn't recall the last time I had been out with my female friends, so I was unusually positive about going to dinner for Jayne's birthday. Of course, I always loved seeing Jayne, and I did enjoy good food, and good company, but dressing up and makeup and taxis and hangovers usually overrode any feelings of excitement. But I needed this and, as I put on my favourite long, loose black dress and attempted a smoky eye, I even felt good about the way I looked. A lot of the time I hardly considered it, these days. And to be honest, I was happy that way. But it is good for the soul to shake things up, sometimes. Not to settle too comfortably into rhythms and routines.

I finished getting ready, but it was early, so I poured myself a gin and tonic, adding a squeeze of lime from a brittle, plastic bottle. I stood at the counter in the kitchen, imagining you getting ready to go out on that fatal night, as I did, with reverence, every single time that I did the same. I imagined you drinking cheap beer from a stubby bottle in the hotel room. I saw you putting on your uncharacteristically knee-length dress, straightening your blonde bob, adding a touch of shimmer to your cheeks. I saw Daniel downing his beer in a few gulps, putting on his expensive-too-warm jeans, and spraying himself with aftershave. I imagined you smiling at him, content, tanned skin touched by the beach sun that day.

It is remarkable how little we know of what will befall us in life. We make plans, behave as if we have some sort of control, strategy, will - but really, everything rests comfortably in the laps of the Gods, until they decide whether to lift us up or throw us down. Throw us. Let us drop.

I suppose you had already talked about what you would do the next day, the days after, when you would be frequenting certain restaurants or sites. More than this, much more, you and Daniel had talked of marriage, Jack had said. And no doubt you still hoped for children. I know you wanted to advance your career; had vague thoughts of exhibiting your own art, or at least taking more drawing classes at the local college. So many things, supposed plans, dreams, passions, ideas, swept away by one little slip. One little push. Or one little fall.

The doorbell rang, showing that my lift had arrived. I downed the remains of my drink and blew you a kiss in the air.

***

There were five of us out for dinner. The restaurant was busy, dim, and cosy and smelt strongly of garlic. It was an old-fashioned place, with no pretensions. Perfect for tonight. I was relieved to find I felt comfortable. We had gone straight to the table – no loitering by the bar or attempting to balance on stools – and the music was not so loud that it drowned out our conversation but was loud enough to generate an atmosphere.

The waiter was flirtatious and jovial with us, each in turn. He asked who the birthday girl was, and then declared her the most beautiful woman at the table. From anyone else, this type of banter could have risked an ear bashing – especially from Jayne -- but the kitsch, well-rehearsed ridiculousness of his patter kept us all in good humour, if gently bored when it went on a touch too long. When he took Marie's order, he told her that her French accent made her sound angelic; when he took Julie's order, she was informed she had the best taste; Carolyn was advised she must be someone's younger sister; I was told he had saved the best for last, as I was his favourite. He somehow managed not to step over the line into leeriness or discomfort. It was quite clear he used the same vapid lines on every table - and that anyone of us could hammer him into shape if we needed to.

I was sitting with Jayne beside me, and Carolyn to my left, making the head of the table. We had done a little dance between chairs when we arrived as we discussed whether Jayne should be sitting at the top, but then realising that Carolyn should be there as she had some hearing loss, and this worked best for her. I was happy with the way the arrangement had turned out – Carolyn was witty and irreverent, and I hadn't seen Jayne since the fundraiser.

The starters were accompanied by cocktails and embarrassing stories from Julie about Jayne's younger years: her disastrous home haircuts and the seventeenth birthday when she had tried to blame her copious vomiting the next day on some bad shellfish.

Between courses, I caught up with Carolyn about school. She still worked at St Ewald's – her first and only teaching job. She had a small additional responsibility of mentoring new staff and supporting others who were struggling, amongst other things - but essentially, she loved being a classroom teacher. She told me about building upgrades, the practice of the current Head, the last set of school results and the latest administrative burdens being put upon them all. She spoke with enthusiasm and affection. It almost made me miss the place. It made me nostalgic about teaching.

"Are you working at all, Catherine?" she asked. "I mean, I know you're retired but I also know what a Trojan you are. I can't imagine you sitting around doing nothing."

"No, not working, but I have been considering volunteering work, lately."

It was true, I had flitting moments when this appealed. Structure and responsibility might not be a bad thing. Though it was the first time I had voiced it aloud. I surprised myself to hear the words fully formed.

"That's a great idea!" Jayne interrupted.

I turned to her and smiled.

"You think everything is a great idea." I teased.

"You've got a lot of skills, and let's face it, a fair amount of time on your hands."

"Cheeky… Did I tell you that my ex is doing supply teaching?"

"Ugh," Carolyn's face said it all. "That's not the sort of thing I'd be advocating."

"Not sure the stress is worth the payoff" said Jayne. "Unless of course you come to work in a school with wonderful staff and discipline, such as mine."

"I'll have a good think about it," I said, insincerely.

The cocktails had merged into wine. Faces were getting blurred and sloppy, windows steamed up with exuberance and food. I struggled to finish my linguine, full as I was with garlic bread, laughter, and Shiraz. Jayne leaned into me, conspiratorially. She moved carefully: even her words were dawdling.

"I don't think I told you, I made a fool of myself."

"Which time?" I teased.

She pulled a face. Her lips were marked purple by the wine, shocking against her pale skin.

"That Eve girl," she said. "You know?"

"No, I don't think I do. Eve who?"

"The nail woman!" There was a slight wail to her voice, unlike her usual composure. "Eve."

"Oh, her! Made a fool? How, exactly?"

"God, can't you guess?" she slumped and looked down onto the table, patterned now with sauce and parmesan cheese. "Don't make me say it."

"You mean… romantically?"

I pictured Eve, her delicate face poking out from her hood at me on my doorstep, birdlike.

"Sort of," she said.

"Sort of," I echoed. "… Could you be a bit more specific, perhaps?"

"Right, let me think. Well, she was coming around about once a month and then one night she asked if she could reschedule and come late, eight o'clock or something. When she arrived, she was frazzled and stressed out. Some issues with a client threatening all sorts of wild and unnecessary things. She was shaken up. Completely thrown by it. I… gave her a cup of tea and managed to calm her down. She started on my nails and one thing led to another and… God."

"What?" I asked, intrigued. I recalled Eve's odd demeanour when I had mentioned Jayne. "What did you do?"

Jayne snapped her head up and looked at me.

"I didn't do anything. I just… I just invited her out. I didn't plan to, but we were getting on well and… well, somehow it just seemed… O.K."

"Ouch. She turned you down, I take it?"

"Well, no, actually. She said yes, at first. She was silent for almost a minute after I said it – something rubbish about seeing her outside of work and would she like to join me for dinner. Or whatever. And she had my left hand held still and flat using the fingers of one hand to keep me steady…" Jayne mimicked the movement with her own hands. "She had the brush of the polish poised in the air, ready to paint my index finger. And she just… froze. I could feel both our hands getting warmer and even a little pulse from her thumb. It was incredibly romantic. And painful. Because I knew – I thought I knew - when she broke the silence, it was going to be a no. So I didn't really want her to speak. I wanted the silence. And the handholding."

"You make it sound very dramatic."

Jayne grimaced. "Kind of, but –"

"But then," I interjected. "She actually said yes. You said she said yes?"

Jayne nodded.

"Literally that. Yes. And then she carried on with my nails. We chatted comfortably and when she left, we held each other's hands again and had a very fleeting, chaste kiss."

"Well, that doesn't sound too bad at all. When do we get to the embarrassing part?"

"The next day. I got up to a text from her. She said she should never have accepted my invitation and that she was sorry to let me down, but she couldn't go to dinner with me after all. I felt ludicrous, this gorgeous woman – I mean, you've seen her - me asking her out like that. I don't even think she is gay."

"Why are you convinced this is so awful? It sounds to me like she liked you too, but she got cold feet. Either she's already spoken for, or she's not sure about going... down that path."

"Going down that path," Jayne repeated, and then frowned. "I think it hurt my pride. I felt old and ugly. Oh, God. Am I some awful letchy, hideous woman?"

She looked at me, pleadingly. I gave a swift shake of the head.

"Well, and the worst of it is, she won't answer my messages – and I'm only after frigging Gels! I haven't had my nails done in weeks. Look at the state of me!"

She held up her hands, black polish chipped, missing altogether from one thumb.

"Priorities!" I laughed. "She… she was a bit young though," I said, cautiously.

"A bit," she said. "But not as young as you'd think. She's about to turn thirty, she told me. And I know I'm moving rapidly towards old age, but I'm not past it yet, myself."

"Oh!" I was surprised. "No, then. Not that much younger." I sipped from my glass. "Thirty is quite grown up."

Jayne raised a glass, then realised it was almost empty. She topped up both of ours, generously.

"Cheers!" she said. "Here's to growing old disgracefully."

We both took a slug of our wine. I put one arm around her and rocked her in a half hug. We pushed our foreheads together, firmly.

"You know, she rather reminded me of Susie," I said.

I had not intended to say this out loud, and the sentence was soft, tentative. Her name hung in a little bubble in the air. "Susie," I said again, more loudly. It popped.

"Yeah," said Jayne. "Me too."

I was processing this reply when Carolyn leaned toward us and said, "What did you say? Are we drinking to Susie? I'll drink to that."

She picked up her glass and said confidently, "To Susie. My good friend's darling, beautiful daughter."

"To Susie," we said, clinking glasses.

"Such an awful, random thing," Carolyn said, almost to herself.

"It's hard to understand," Jayne said.

"Hmm. Yes and no," Carolyn answered.

"What do you mean?" I asked. "Yes, and no?" I couldn't gauge her tone.

"I… I'm so sorry, Catherine. That didn't sound right. I didn't mean to speak out of turn. I don't mean anything really; just that yes, it's hard to process it. It must be incredibly hard to… what's the word? Recalibrate, I guess? You, and your family, I mean."

"Re-cal-ur-bray-te," muttered Jayne, beside me.

Carolyn glanced at her but carried on.

"But, well, likewise, life is a bastard, isn't it? These random, stupid, hurtful things do just happen. Often. There's no rhyme or reason. It's shit. So, we don't ever think things will happen to us. But they happen all the time. All the bloody time. Just slips and accidents."

"Just slips and accidents," Jayne said, nodding.

"Yes," I said. "Accidents just happen."

I started to pile our plates up together, scraping the left-over pizza crusts and oily sauces into one congealed, rich mess and brushing crumbs into my palm.

Our dessert arrived and I was glad of the respite. I had no idea why I had ordered anything, as I hadn't finished my main course and I was already thinking about my taxi home. Before the waiter had even finished placing everyone's fresh plates down, I had asked him to call me a cab; though it was a while before it came, and I had two more rushed drinks before the manager came over to indicate it was outside.

***

I woke wearing an old t-shirt, with a pile of jewellery and a glass of water beside my bed. I could smell my own breath: rich and sour with garlic, herbs, and dehydration. It was only seven o'clock, and I was irritated that I felt both tired and wide awake. I don't think I've slept in beyond eight since I turned forty.

I went to the kitchen, downed a fresh glass of chilled water, and prepared a cafetière of coffee. Then I went straight into the shower while the kettle boiled. I was vaguely disappointed with myself and felt that familiar mix of embarrassment and self-doubt, where I wondered why I had not exercised moderation, and whether I had done or said anything awful. Like Sophie, her horror at experiencing a hangover. But sadly, I'd lost count of how many I'd had. I wondered if you ever had that feeling, sensitive as you were. That sinking, dark feeling associated with knowing better, and not having acted your age. I hoped not.

By the time I was washing my hair, I was chuckling to myself about various anecdotes, and the rousing rendition of Happy Birthday we had provided when Jayne's coffee arrived, with a tiny cupcake holding one candle.

On balance, it had been fun, and worth it.

Wrapped in a bathrobe, I grabbed my phone from my handbag, poured myself a coffee and opened the patio doors, standing in the cool air to blast away still more of last night's fug. I placed my drink on the garden table and checked my messages. Two: one from Jack, saying he planned to call this evening, and another from a number that I didn't know.

It was Carolyn: *Hey, Catherine. Hope this is still ur number? Just to let u know that J took a tumble when she left the restaurant last night. Marie took her to A and E. She's fine! Turns out she sprained her ankle badly and a couple of bruises. Sounds like they had to wait there hours though, poor things. Thought u would want to knw! Carolyn x*

That sounded like a rather deflating end to the evening for them; I texted Carolyn back to say so.

Yeh, and I think she'll be embarrassed today and might not be in touch, but she could need looking after so thought I'd tell u. I'll pop to see her this eve. Slips and accidents, eh? It's a shame. X x I guess it will make a classic story, some day.

Yes. It's surprising how easily these things happen X x, I texted back.

She tried to shut the door, but they were still intertwined, and he had a flip-flopped foot, a hand, an elbow in the way. They laughed into each other's faces. She could see the bridge of his nose, the filaments of bristle on his upper lip. There was the sour tang of lager as he leaned in, to kiss her again.

She pushed against the door edge; he squeezed out of the way, shuffling himself around without extricating himself from the embrace.

"You big softie," she said.

She leapt away from him, taking two steps further into the hotel room as she turned, twisting in a fractured pirouette, dancing for him, playfully, coquettishly. She kicked off her sandals.

Her bare feet skidded on the tiles as she raced towards the balcony, then yanked the sliding doors open, enough to squeeze through.

She was almost on the other side, one hand still on the handle, and he was there. His hands were there. A forearm tanned, hairs sun-bleached and frazzled, skin glowing with sun, hunger. Beautiful. Warm. Large fingers, imposingly large, were searching to grasp her arms, her torso, her clothes until she could not feel the doorframe anymore. She could not feel the evening breeze. She could not feel anything but this.

She was staggering backwards now. Staggering backwards, as they locked together in one; her tongue seeking his, his great hands over her clothes, pressing. And she was transported in the air; pictured dandelion clocks ready to explode in the wind.

They fell into a tight embrace, and stood together, sealed in a tangle of limbs for a full minute. She felt the comfort and reassurance of him. She turned herself around without breaking the lock of his fingers, until he stood behind her, with his arms around her waist.

"I could stare at this view for hours," she said. And it was true.

"It is wonderful," he said. "But I need a shower. I feel greasy and tired. I'm sorry, sweetheart."

"Ate too much, you mean."

"There's no such thing."

He kissed her on the top of the head, gave her a quick squeeze and then stepped away. She stayed still. She could still feel the pressure of his hands. His body, his kiss at various points across her skin. She revelled in it. The bathroom door gaped and then crashed against the wall in the distance; she breathed in the warmth of the night. The breeze lifted the scent of mint and chlorine up towards her.

She leant forward to try to see the view between the rooftops. She felt her shins against the cool surface, the feeling creeping up her legs, her hips, as she pushed further against the short wall. She was at the edge of the balcony. In the distance, she could hear low singing through the water of a shower.

As she stood, face in the wind, she caught a familiar figure from the corner of her eye. He had come out onto his balcony in the next block and then gone in again. Wet trunks now hung and dripped from the broken drying rail.

She called out to him. She knew it was futile; she was nervous to shout too loudly; it was late. He would never have heard her.

For a second, she felt light-headed, as if hit by vertigo. Perhaps she was tipsier than she had realised. She took a step back and shook herself. The moment passed.

Between the buildings, in the distance, she thought she saw Jessica, standing in the shadows, talking to a man – who was *that? She leant further forwards, her body arching steeply over the edge, as far as she could, while holding the top of the balcony, curiosity getting the better of her. She lifted one arm as if to wave, and then realised how foolish that would be.*

Then she felt the toes on her right foot touch something damp; her foot slipping, sliding, rapidly, then her left-hand buckling beneath her as her body jerked down violently. Her elbow could not hold her weight. The top half of her body lurched over the balcony, her right arm that had begun to wave was hanging down, her head bobbing ineptly, her legs split at an ungainly angle. She tried to straighten up and her foot slipped again. The wall was low. Too low. She tried to grab it but overshot and found her fingers lacing the air on the other side. What was happening?

She sensed a sea of panic flood her as she realised, she could not stop this. Her body was in motion, propelling over. Tumbling. She could not stop.

It happened so quickly. It just happened.

She cried out. Cartwheeled her arms.

And then she fell.

Chapter 26

Do you remember when Jack broke his leg? How useless he was at resting, keeping still? You would have been in your element: reading, drinking tea, enjoying the fuss we would have made of you even when you were the slightest bit sick. The boys used to laugh at how I indulged this side of you. You did like to be waited on and looked after as a child; childhood illnesses read about in classic children's novels gave you romanticised pretentions of what influenza and the measles might be like, I think.

Jack, however, was bitter that he could not Go-Kart for his friend's birthday; go to rugby practice on a Sunday; or ride his bike on the road in front of the house. Well, Jayne was much the same. She insisted on coming to help me with painting the hallway, even though she still had a limp and a bandage.

"Are you sure this is how you are going to want to spend your Saturday?" I asked. "I imagine it's the last thing I would have wanted to volunteer for when I was still working in the school."

"We always help each other with decorating," she said. "It's our thing."

"And is it 'our thing' even when one of us has made a recent trip to A&E?" I asked.

"Yes," she replied. "It's always our thing."

"Well, I got through quite a lot of it over the last few days, but I made sure to leave you the skirting boards. Nothing that requires balance or gross motor skills."

"Ha bloody ha," she answered. "Unless you are planning to feed me Cosmopolitans and red wine, turn all the lights off and make me try to walk on a broken pavement in heels, then my balance should be just fine."

"Damn. I shall have to cancel several bookings now," I teased. "Though actually, I did think we might tuck into the red wine afterwards. I've not had anything since your fateful night."

"Oh yes, of course," she laughed. "When the cutting in and what-not is all safely done and dusted. No wobbly-edged hallways for you, missus."

"O.K. so see you tomorrow. Around ten-thirty?"

***

The next day I woke with a jolt, thinking I had heard a clatter but unsure where from. I had been dreaming heavy, cotton-wool dreams again, the type where I am condensed down, concentrated, until I am nothing but your mother. Nothing but yours. And I am lost and confused and desperate. Searching for something, unsure what it is; or searching for you, unsure why.

I needed coffee.

I had breakfast first, and then dressed in an old black t-shirt, which was now – I noticed with a sting – a little too small, and a pair of leggings. I pushed my hair back with an unflattering Alice band and went out to check the post.

Immediately outside my door, on my doorstep was a small mound of rubbish: a banana skin, some potato peelings, a teabag. I stood in it, barefoot, and felt the decomposing matter turn to sludge under my weight: wet sand between my toes. The teabag had burst, and a small eruption of brown mire added to the composting litter. I had a moment of complete confusion while I stared at it, unable to comprehend what was happening, having been moving automatically until that point. Then I glanced around the lobby area of the flats, to see if this was part of a wider scene. It was localised to my front door. This was good because there was less to clean up, but also very bad, as this probably meant it must have been placed there intentionally. For me.

My heart sank.

I stepped over the mess and walked to collect my mail. In the little pigeon-hole was another mound of rubbish – some used tinfoil, a chocolate bar wrapper, a little hillock of torn and stained receipts. Tentatively, I picked one up. It was a receipt for the Italian restaurant from Jayne's birthday meal. Mine. I dropped it and rushed to the front door to go outside.

The flats' bins were located through a little archway to the side of the front door, through an old wooden gate. An idle passer-by wouldn't know they were there. Only the residents – and presumably a few of their guests – would. Unless they watched, of course. Unless they watched someone's movements from afar, in secret.

I tripped down the cold stairs outside, grimy of foot and ill-prepared for public view, but impatient. On the steps, I spotted a few drops of dried yoghurt, a cashew nutshell, a piece of notepaper torn small and serrated as a stamp: small specks of intimacy and domesticity that pocked the way between the front door and the entrance. I creaked open the black gate to see the bins, exactly as they usually were - except for mine, tilted over, the contents strewn around the floor in a riot of colour and smells.

***

By the time Jayne arrived, a little late as she had not accounted for the hobbling and wobbling required, I was on my third cup of coffee. In front of me, I had the receipt, smoothed out into a snakeskin of paper. Everything else had been bagged up into a new bin liner and put back. I'm not sure why I kept this one thing, or what clue it might give. I had been staring at it for a full fifteen minutes before she arrived.

I let Jayne in and went straight back to my seat, after grabbing a mug for her and placing it opposite me. When I caught sight of her, her tentative footsteps turning her into a puppet, I felt guilty that I had charged ahead of her, oblivious, not offering to help or at least showing empathy by moving slowly.

"I'm sorry I'm late," she said. "It's a pain in the backside, not being fully mobile... I thought you might have started, to be honest. Glad you haven't though. I do need this coffee."

"I'm not exactly moving at my fastest today, either. Something nasty has happened."

It was the first time I had told anyone about the odd things that had been taking place, except the boys next door – and even then, I hadn't bothered filling them in on the recent things – the squashed flower beds, the rubbish. I felt daft telling her about the litter: it sounded petty, and paranoid, once I voiced it out loud. So I added in about the graffiti by my doorbell for good measure. I couldn't bring myself to go through each chapter of events, but these two things seemed spiteful and targeted enough to be connected. I told her how the word had been scratched in jagged, bitter writing, and how the rubbish had been placed only at my door, and only in with my mail.

Jayne was frowning with a tight pinch between her eyebrows.

"A stalker then? You think you might have a stalker?"

"I... not... I mean, I haven't been getting phone calls, love letters, or threats," I attempted a joke. "Not sure which would be worse!"

Jayne ignored this.

"Horrid though. Might be worth reporting."

She stated it – it wasn't really a question.

"It's just unsettling. I'm... unnerved. And you know, I don't scare easily. Not if I can help it, anyway. There's no point worrying about things that might not be real or might never happen."

"I wish I was like that. Anyway, I suppose it might just be a coincidence. Someone pissed, thinking they are being funny or intimidating or something. Maybe you have inadvertently annoyed them somehow. And the graffiti thing. That could be unconnected, right? You said it was a while ago. It could just be kids... Actually, come to think of it, the rubbish could just be urban foxes, or gulls or something," she shuddered. "Rats."

"But foxes wouldn't bring the rubbish into the hallway and place it on top of my post."

"No," she considered. "But if someone was miffed that your bin was over – maybe they thought you'd overfilled it or hadn't shut it or something – well, perhaps they would have blamed you for the wildlife getting in. Wanted to make a point."

"That does seem like a more rational explanation."

"But the stuff being on your doorstep, and in with your post. That is quite... personal. Your own rubbish at your own door... weird. Is the exterior door always shut? Have you ever found it left open when you've come home?"

"Very rarely. If someone is running out to their car or something. Never overnight, in my experience."

"What are your neighbours like?" she said, in a stage whisper, jerking her head towards the wall.

I laughed.

"Delightful. It's not them."

She looked disappointed.

"Your bin has your flat number on?"

"Yes."

We both fell silent for a moment and drank the remnants of our coffee, almost cold as it was.

"Any idea, then? Who might be doing it? If it is someone, I mean."

"No, I… I can't think of anyone."

I pictured Sebastien; the journalist David Jones - or at least, how I imagined he looked; Daniel. They crowded in on me, and yet the idea that it could be any of them was absurd. Was I losing my mind, myself? Turning into some doddery, obsessive woman, with too much time on my hands? Too much time to dwell, introspectively, until somehow, I imagined myself important enough that it is all about me. Everything.

It was ludicrous to think I was important enough – intimidating enough – to anyone that they would target me in that way.

"Right," I said, slapping my thighs with both hands to indicate it was time to move on from this. "Let's get on with this painting."

"Are you sure?" Jayne asked.

"Quite sure," I said. "I'll keep an eye on the front door over the next few weeks, and I'll ask the other residents if they'd be happy to get a lock on the gate for the alleyway. I've already fitted a sensor light and some bolts on the doors, I did that a few weeks back."

"Really?"

She was looking at me, trying to judge my mood, I guessed.

"Yes. Better to be safe than sorry. But honestly, I'm not that rattled."

"Ever my practical friend," Jayne said, head tilted, smiling up at me.

***

When your dad and I divorced, I allowed you to choose your own decoration for your rooms. Jack was not interested: proclaiming that he wanted a double bed and plain walls, and as he was getting older, off to uni, it wasn't long until he was rarely there, anyway. I can't say that it ever felt like his bedroom, or that the house ever felt like it was his home. You, on the other hand, were overjoyed. You spent hours flicking through magazines and looking at photos of glamorous homes on the internet. We started storing up items for your room in the hall cupboard: knick-knacks and bargain cushions that we found on our shopping trips. By the time everything had gone through court, and we had moved, your taste had shifted a little. Children grow up quickly. You were too polite to say – knowing the time and money invested in those purchases – but I did spot that some of the items stayed relegated to the hallway, or under your bed.

Now, I was painting everything white. You'll remember the colour of my hallway? A pale lemon. It had been that way for years. When I first painted it, I thought it was so chirpy; you liked it too. But now it looked old-fashioned and tired. I had a new, inexpensive lampshade ready to go up, in dark blue, to replace the glass one that had been there since I first moved in. I could already see how much cleaner and fresher the space looked. I was going to focus in on the details as I knew you would – with your artist's eye. Change the light switches and door handles.

I was doing it in order to put Jessica's prints up and to do them justice.

We painted until mid-afternoon, happily finishing just as my head started to fill with the haze of fumes. I realised that although we'd had a tea break at around midday, I had not stopped to make us a sandwich as promised – we had worked straight through, chatting happily, and working diligently. She told me all sorts of stories that I had not heard before about her family, mainly. I wondered how self-absorbed I must have been for these tales never to have surfaced before. Some were recent family traumas and mini tragedies that she had failed to mention.

"Hungry?" I asked as we cleaned the oily brushes at the kitchen sink.

"Ravenous," Jayne answered. "Fancy an early dinner? Takeaway?"

"Yes, to the food, no to the takeaway," I said. "I'll cook."

Jayne perched herself back on her stool and drank tap water while I started to chop vegetables.

"Did I tell you that I've been invited to Daniel's thirtieth?" I offered.

"Daniel?" she asked, "*The* Daniel?"

"No other."

"Blimey," she said. "You guys are… are real friends these days, are you?"

"No. Not friends. But it is getting better. Or I am, anyway… I think."

"Well, that's cleared that up."

I laughed.

"I think I just need to treat him in a normal way. Be normal. Stop thinking of him so differently from everyone else Susie knew. I have this peculiar sort of… mantle that falls over all my thoughts about him. That stops me from thinking clearly. Makes everything odd and vague. There's no reason for it. Nothing logical, anyway. But it shouldn't be… It's quite simple. He was there on holiday with her when she – Susie – when… well, that doesn't make him much more culpable than anyone else who was with her. Than anyone else who was there."

"I guess that's true."

"So, I need to finish this obsession of mine and see things clearly. And just treat him like I would anyone else. Besides, it's not good for me to allow myself to think and feel otherwise. It's not exactly been working out for me that well so far."

"That sounds very sensible," Jayne said.

"You know me," I said, taking two wine glasses from the cupboard.

Chapter 27

One of my favourite pictures of you is the selfie you took on the night after your graduation. You are a little out of focus, face tilted, mouth wide, teeth straight, eyes closed. Your hair is falling loose into the air behind, with you arching back with laughter – your body following your head. With one arm around you, Jessica is just in shot, in profile, looking at you and grinning. In the background is a gaggle of other students, laughing, pointing, waving, dancing.

I wasn't there that night, of course. It doesn't hold any specific memory for me. But you look joyous. The blur of your movement, your arching, artless openness, makes you seem almost ethereal. As if we are seeing you through a diaphanous veil, or clouds.

I was waiting in the kitchen for a taxi to collect me to take me to the party, thinking of you as I sipped my tea. I checked my social media and 'liked' some posts of Sandra's, posting a quick '*wishing you both much luck x*' beneath her latest announcement, where they were just a few hundred pounds from her fundraising target. Things seemed to be looking up for them, and with his health. I was relieved.

I wondered if you had spent long getting ready that night of the picture – had you sat on the floor cross-legged in front of your full-length mirror, teasing your hair and applying eyeliner? Or had you been bundled up into your clutch of friends all day, bouncing with excitement and dread that it was finally over; you had finished university.

Your father and I had been at the ceremony, had cheered when you had walked across the stage, hatted, and robed, and stood with you in the sun outside The Great Hall, taking dozens of photographs and snatching hugs. But we had left by mid-afternoon, both of us getting the same, packed train, and my suspicion was that you had spent the rest of the day hopping from café to pub, chatting, snacking, and drinking with your friends. I hoped so.

My phone bleeped to tell me the taxi was outside. It was time to go.

***

I had never been to the restaurant where the party was held before, and it was more modest, and cosier than I had expected. In fact, it was lovely. The building was historical, old – nineteenth century, at an uneducated guess – with low ceilings and granite walls. The furniture was mismatched wood, and each room was full of candles, artfully dripping, wax sculpted into squat gothic torches. In the function room, there was even a huge iron candelabra along one of the wooden beams above us. A large wood burner was in the corner of the bar. As I approached the function room to the rear of the building, a heady mix of herbs, spices and fruits filled the place, promising an eclectic fusion of food: cumin, basil, lemon, garlic.

A waiter took my coat and hung it on a rack as I glanced through the archway into the space. There were only twenty or so people milling around, sedately, so far. I couldn't see Jessica, yet.

My phone bleeped again: a message from Sandra Smith, wishing me luck. I smiled – she would know how I was feeling, and I appreciated the moral support.

I had taken a few steps in, when a young man came over to me with a tray of sparkling wine, one of which I happily took. I was glancing around, looking for a place to leave my present, when Sophie appeared.

"Hi!" she said enthusiastically. "I'm so glad you came. Daniel will be thrilled."

"It's nice to see you again," I replied. "You look lovely."

She did – in that she was wearing a pretty, knee-length dress, tied by a ribbon under her bust, with loose, chiffon sleeves. But she also looked a little tired, pinched, I realised. The whites of her eyes were slightly pink, and she had a little pattern of spots on her chin.

She shrugged. "I've got a bit of a dicky tummy, actually. Don't worry, not a hangover this time." She laughed. "And nothing contagious, either. Something I ate."

Daniel rushed over and placed one arm around her waist.

"Catherine. I am so, so glad you came."

His smile was wide and warm. He leant in to kiss me on one cheek. He turned towards Sophie.

"O.K. now, sweetheart? Are you feeling alright?"

His voice was quiet and tender, spoken into her ear. She nodded.

"Hey, look who's just walked in," he pronounced.

I turned to see Jessica striding over. She wore the same fitted black dress she had been in on the day I met her at the exhibition, but this time it was paired with high-heeled ankle boots covered in little chains and beads. Her hair was loose – it had been some time since I had seen her with her hair down and I was surprised by how long it was, and how youthful she looked.

"Wow!" Daniel cried. "You look amazing."

He turned to Sophie and pulled an apologetic face, but she gave a little chuckle, unbothered.

"Hi," I said, leaning towards her and grabbing her forearm, pulling her forwards to me so that she sped up, reached me more quickly. "This is Sophie."

"Hi! Great to meet you. And you, birthday boy. Long time no see."

They stood and looked at each other for a beat, faces inscrutable. Then Jessica leapt forwards and encompassed him in her arms, her silver handbag sliding down her arm as they rocked together in a full and tight embrace. The bag swung hypnotically from its long strap as a pendulum, almost hitting the floor. I watched it, counting the beats. When they broke away, Daniel's eyes were gleaming. Damp.

"Let's get you a glass of something," he said, looking around and behind him for the waiter. "Do you want anything, Sophie?"

"No, thank you. I couldn't handle another glass of orange juice."

"Well. I guess you'll have to have a Prosecco then," said Jessica.

Sophie smiled. "Sounds like it could be fun… but I'm not drinking. Don't worry about me."

It was a tiny, almost imperceptible thing that happened next – and I wondered, later, if I had imagined it – but I saw Daniel's eyes dart back to her, from over her shoulder where he was trying to catch the eye of the server. He glanced back and then down to her belly. Then he walked past her towards the waiter, and as he did so he stroked her stomach gently, swiftly: one, two, with his left hand – ruffling her dress which she quickly wafted out and loose again so that her shape was lost under the fabric and folds.

My cheeks stung and a strange, cold sweat prickled my forehead. As if I had been slapped by a damp towel.

Sophie looked up at me and frowned.

"I'm just going to see when the food will be out," she said. "Why don't you guys grab those seats while you have the chance?"

She waved over to some high-backed velvet chairs in the corner.

"Good call," said Jessica. "Come on, Catherine. Best be quick."

When Daniel found us again, he had a fresh drink for me, and I downed what was left of the one I had. He left us to it, promising to come back to catch up with Jessica later. I sat back in my chair, relieved that I felt protected and hidden by its wings.

Jessica chatted away, seemingly oblivious to my discomfort, periodically slowing down her happy babble as she scanned the room, recognising various people or wondering if she knew others. She pointed out Daniel's parents to me and two friends of hers who I didn't recall. She told me about the new painting she had started, and about her work with the charity. She spoke at length about an exciting new venture she was considering, and I could sense that she was hoping I would approve of it, so I allowed her to speak uninterrupted, as I smiled keenly and concentrated on slowing my breathing. After a little while, I was calm again.

We went to get some food, and I had a pleasant exchange at the buffet table with some of Daniel's colleagues. They thought highly of him, speaking with a touch of awe. I piled my plate high with hummus and tagine, and little feta cheese pastry pockets. There were even small, hard 'dakos' – Cretan appetisers with tomato and olive oil. He must have asked for them specifically.

After everyone had eaten and the little that was left of the food was being cleared away, a young man I didn't recognise tinkled a glass with a spoon and indicated speeches. Then Daniel's father said a few words about the difficult times he had experienced, how proud he was of the man he had become, and how lucky they were to have such a generous son. Next, Daniel stepped forward.

"All I want to say, literally, is 'thank you'. Thank you all for coming. And thank you for being such wonderful friends and family. Cheers." He raised his glass high and around the room everyone murmured and smiled and took a deep sip of their drinks.

The two men hugged and stood with their arms wrapped around each other, as Daniel's friend gave a toast to him. Daniel's mum held hands with Sophie. It was very touching.

Jessica found me again and we managed to locate two stools and place them next to each other at the bar. The atmosphere was now relaxed, voices rising, laughter in the air. I hadn't drunk anything since the two drinks when I'd arrived, which was well over an hour and a half ago now, and I happily accepted Jessica's suggestion of a gin and tonic. The evening had not been so awful, and I felt a sense of relief start to overtake me, as I realised the worst was over. I was ordering a second round of drinks and considering asking where the closest taxi rank was, as it was now, almost, an acceptable time to leave, when I felt a tap on my shoulder.

"You're the mum of his ex, right? He said you're her mum."

A squat, broad young man in a shiny navy-blue suit was facing me. There was a stain on his lapel and a small damp patch on his chin. I wasn't sure if it was drink or drool. He was pointing vaguely behind him with one hand, a near-empty, brown beer bottle, in the other.

"His ex?" I said. "No. I think you have the wrong person."

I started to turn back towards the bar. His tapping persisted, then turned to a light grip over my right shoulder. He tried to pull me back around again.

"Hey!" cried Jessica.

"You are! Dan said. That Sophie girl he was with."

"Sophie is still his girlfriend. She's right there."

Jessica pointed to Sophie with one arm, simultaneously snatching his other arm away from me in a well-timed dance.

He shook his head and groaned.

"Not *that* Sophie! The other one…"

He crunched his eyes for a moment and tapped at his head to bring your name back.

"Susie!" he proclaimed proudly.

"So not Sophie at all then." Jessica rolled her eyes. "Women all the same to you, I guess," she muttered to herself.

She looked at me, and we locked eyes. Then she raised her voice and spoke more firmly.

"We're trying to have a drink and catch up here, love. Could you give us some space?"

He stayed still and acted as if she had not spoken. The drop of fluid on his chin was starting to spread and roll down, forming a miniature map of Italy. He was grinning at me. I did not speak.

"Were you alike?" he asked, with a slight slur.

I didn't answer. He took a step forward until the toe of his right shoe was pressing against the leg of my stool. I could feel the pressure on it, threatening to tip the stool back, threatening to topple me over. He leant in, even closer. I could sense the dank heat of him. A salty, musty warmth.

"Are you a party girl, too?"

I pushed my torso away from him, leaning hard into the back of my seat, but thrusting my arms forwards with both hands knotted together, to block him. He stayed where he was, too close. I gave him a gentle shove: still, he didn't move back, though he wobbled.

"Could you give me some space, please?" My teacher voice resurfaced.

"Oh… I think maybe you are!" he cried; eyebrows raised. "I like them… feisty!"

Jessica jumped off her stool and attempted to crawl into the little space there was left between us.

"Hey, that's enough," I heard her say.

"Are you wild, then?" he breathed, moist lips up against my cheek, almost touching my skin.

His face smelt of sweat and garlic.

"Eh? Do you like it risky, too? Like it dangerous, eh?"

I was falling down into myself. My emotions dropping, words were gone, and I was plunging, picturing you. Picturing a man like him. A faceless man, wanting you, naming you, taking you. Blaming you. This was wrong. This was the story they told of you; even now, here. People who did not know you. They had no right.

We stayed stuck in a tableau, briefly. Him leaning in, the pressure against my flat hands, his wet, wobbly chin and sweat patches. My back arched in my chair. Chin up but head back. Defiant. Anxious. Shocked.

Then he shoved a hand forward, trying to fumble towards my thigh, ineptly, unexpectedly.

He was yanked away of a sudden, and the room was filled with a bellow.

"Jesus, what the hell are you doing?"

It was Daniel's voice, but lower, louder, somehow older. It cut through the party. He had grabbed the young man by one arm, sending his bottle of beer in a splatter through the air until it landed on the floor and heaved out in glugs onto the stone. I stared down at it, trying to allow my thoughts to catch up with the action.

"I said," Daniel repeated. "What the hell do you think you are doing?"

He was tugging him, brusquely, further away from me with each word.

"Whoa, whoa, Dan the man, mate, steady on..."

"Don't you – it's not me who needs to calm the fuck down, 'mate'."

Daniel had him at least two metres away by now. He was still holding his arm. Daniel was the shorter of the two by several inches, but steady on his feet, and stockier. Body taut with anger. Daniel looked at me, a pleading, worried sheen to his eyes.

"O.K.?" he mouthed.

I nodded. I was surprised at how grateful I was to see this.

"I was just chatting to this... to Soph— Susie's mum. Just chatting to the nice lady."

He was trying to twist it into a joke. Trying to defuse it, bat it away as nothing; oblivious to the raw fury of his assailant or the disgust from me and Jessica.

"I don't think she wants to 'chat' anymore. I think it's time you went home and slept everything off."

I glanced around the room; to the rear, some people continued, oblivious, picturesquely illuminated by the soft candlelight. A different scene unfolded a few metres into the room. Faces were turned, most confused, some disgusted. A small group of men stood, leaning forward, ready to leap into any melee that ensued. A teenage girl to my right was staring straight at me, brows arching upwards in concern and squeezing her eyes into triangles.

The young man lurched and twisted, trying to look back at me.

"We were just chatting, eh? Tell him, ladies."

"Will you just piss off?" cried Jessica, as she stepped forward and stood in front of me, arms wide. "He's an arse, Daniel. He needs to leave," she said.

He raised his eyebrows, seemingly amused, then spat, "I wonder if being thick as shit runs in the family. Probably had a lucky escape. What kind of… what kind of stupid ass slag falls from a balcony, anyway?"

He lifted one arm and surveyed the room, with a wobble. Somehow hoping for approval from his audience.

"What did you—"

Daniel's neck was knotted, tendons and veins raised into rope, the skin on his face instantly blotched, red, and white.

"It's... what's it. Thingy. That dude. Darwin, mate... It's natural selection."

He looked remarkably pleased with himself and his wit, carefully annunciating the words.

I went to stand but banged into Jessica. Watching in the gaps between her arms and the back of the young man, between the angles of their limbs, I saw Daniel take one step back and raise his right fist up, high, where he held it, halted; he was shaking with fury, indecisive, lost.

His father cried out – "Daniel!"

Jessica staggered slightly, and my view was broken. Then there was a brief coarse noise, and a gasp, and then I could see that the young man's head was cocked at an unnatural angle now, toppled to the side, though Daniel had not moved. Through the low light of the room strands of saliva like spun sugar were glimmering, streaming from his mouth. A dark pink patch was rising on his cheek, like a scold. I pushed Jessica to one side to see properly. She shuffled across by two steps but remained in the same position, motionless in shock.

In the middle of the two men stood Sophie, one arm slightly raised, her palm flat, fingers pushed tight, together: held firm in the shadow of the fierce slap that she had given him.

Chapter 28

I woke too early, to a full, cold cup of herbal tea and a glass of water by the side of my bed. My lamp had been on all night, and I was chilled, having slept in just an old t-shirt, again. Another new habit? I hoped not. Memories of the night swam into view; the speeches; my assailant; Sophie's slap. I knew there would be messages on my mobile phone: thankfully, I had left it in the kitchen. I needed a moment to process this alone. I lay still for a moment, untangling the unexpected events as they popped one in front of the other in my mind.

Sophie's defence of me – or of you – haunted me the most, and I was unsure why.

I crawled out of bed and straight to the shower to try to shake away the mild hangover I had: brought about by the two (or was it three?) very large whiskies that Jessica and I had downed in the flat after Daniel's father had put us in a taxi home. She was ready to call the police, which at the time had seemed a huge overreaction, but on reflection, perhaps was not.

I was not going to allow the evening to unsettle me. I was not. I was going to reflect on this, but not dwell. Take the best of it and continue to move on. You deserved that: he did not. I decided, mid-shower, to take a trip out on the bus, to walk, and think, and enjoy some unseasonal sunshine.

By ten o'clock I was at the bus station, and fifteen minutes later I was boarding the 12A to Eccleston village.

***

The bus was quiet, which was understandable for a Sunday morning in early winter. I was cold as I boarded, but soon began to warm – the windows steaming up with the heat of the few passengers who got on, and off, along the way. I wiped away a cloud from the glass to allow myself a view as we went deeper into the countryside.

You always found bus journeys exciting as a young child. I know many children do, but your brother had not, so your pure and simple delight always tickled me. The buses we took were inevitably old and noisy, with few soft textures and an interior that was 80 per cent metal. You did not notice. It was the adventure you liked. The possibilities.

The road to Eccleston is a hotchpotch of pretty hamlets and modern villages, with industrial estates flanked by out-of-town supermarkets with tin roofs. In my experience, many people imagine the countryside to be a ubiquitously picturesque place, but clearly not all farms are small, organic family businesses; not all homes are thatched. Far from it. And there can be a harsh contrast in lifestyles and opportunities among those who live there. Rural poverty is brutal because it is rarely acknowledged for what it is.

My mum, Granny, lived in one of those pretty hamlets for the last twenty years of her life, but close enough to a trading estate for her own childhood to remain a living memory. She had come from a single-parent home, with her father having died at a young age. Around your age, in fact. She had very few memories of him. Her mother had worked in a shop, and then as a seamstress, and finally had run her own very small business as a dressmaker. She was somewhat of a pioneer in the area, it seemed, being a courageous woman who managed to steadily increase her skills and her children's opportunities over the decades she was alive. But mum did not forget the earlier years, and she herself always valued plain hard work. She would have been incredibly proud of you; it seemed unjust that your lives did not overlap further.

The bus continued to bounce along the road, stopping less often as we drove further out of town, the houses spaced out, the population slight.

I wondered for a moment what she would have made of Sophie's actions last night. Would she have thought this admirable? Or inappropriate? There was no denying the young man needed chastising - but he was drunk and idiotic. Perhaps we gave him too much credit, taking him seriously. He ended up being the star of the evening when it was Daniel's party. He was an attention seeker, so he got what he wanted, in a way.

I was glad Sophie had done it, and it did not diminish my view of her. At the same time, I always felt uncomfortable with women hitting men; only because I despise men hitting women, so why should it be acceptable the other way around?

And if he had hit her back? Well, all hell would have broken loose.

But then, he was degrading women – me, your memory – so perhaps it was only just that he should have experienced humiliation at the hands of another female. Perhaps this time it was right for a woman to hit a man. Or for anyone to hit him – gender aside, altogether.

I found it hard to reconcile. Granny's wisdom – or even Nanna's – would have come in handy.

A fleeting, previously forgotten memory popped into my head. Daniel and Nanna. I had failed to remember that they had even met until then, but of course they did, at Jack's birthday. We were out for a rare, long, late Sunday lunch, and had all changed seats before the dessert course, at the insistence of your father. It must have been a milestone birthday, for Nanna to be there, and your father, too. But I couldn't recall. I did remember my feelings of irritation at the time, with his control of the situation and the fact I had to relinquish my seat at the head of the table – which I was sure he was eyeing up. He usually had some sort of ulterior motive at play.

Daniel had ended up sat with Nanna from that point onwards. Who knows what they found to talk about, but by the time the coffee arrived, I recall a few elbows nudging and a general sense of amusement around the table when we noticed that they were completing a crossword puzzle together, from a Sunday broadsheet. I still don't know where it had come from, incongruous as it was to the birthday meal, the setting. Jack took a photograph on his phone, and the flash caught Daniel's attention, and he laughed, a genuine, unconscious laugh, as he realised everyone was watching them. You were delighted. Nanna thought he was wonderful.

We weren't far from Eccleston now, and I wondered what time White's would be open on a Sunday, if at all. I was looking forward to coffee and cake, with my hangover still nipping at the edges of me.

I stood, pushed the button, and moved towards the front of the bus.

***

I crossed the road over to the carpark where we usually parked and tried to retrace my steps from the last time I had been there, with Jayne. I wanted to recall exactly what route we had walked – not that there were many options – as we had ended up going awry. Shortly down the path, I realised our error, and I turned left along a muddy bridle path lined with blackberry bushes, musty grey-green pocked with dark purple clusters of over-soft fruit. The odd berry still remained in place, even now, as autumn and winter had been mild so far, and I was tempted to pick one but could hear Granny telling me that the devil would have spoiled them, as it was after Michaelmas.

Daniel is surprisingly superstitious too, isn't he? I remember watching him throw salt over one shoulder without missing a beat in his conversation, staring at him, fascinated, as he did so without comment. This modern, stylish young man with this illogical mannerism. You teased him for it, each time he did it – which was surprisingly frequently - and he accepted it, made some sort of silly joke about it being bad luck to be superstitious, tapping his head to touch wood. I could picture you, laughing, grabbing his hand, and kissing his fingertips while he pulled a face.

You did love each other.

And now he loved Sophie. That much was clear to see. Funny really, that I struggled to think of him moving on, when of course you two were fairly unlikely to have remained a duo for life. In spite of Jack's revelation about possible engagements or wedding plans, which had not yet come to anything and may only have been the vaguest of plans for all I knew. And you were both still young. It was entirely possible that you would have broken up naturally, even if the accident had not occurred. Or you had survived. He could have ended up with Sophie, even if you were alive.

I was back around, having walked my loop. I was hoping that White's tearoom would be open now, as it was lunchtime. I caught myself crossing the fingers on my hand and laughed. Daniel would have approved. But there was no call for wishes or magic – the place was open, and the very same table I had just recently sat at with Jayne, was free.

The tearoom was fairly busy, but they were happy enough to accommodate me at my requested table although it could easily have sat four. I made a point of changing seats, placing myself where Jayne had sat so as not to feel too ridiculous at my own desire for repetition and familiarity. I peeled off my scarf and felt my hair begin to stick to the back of my neck, hit by the humidity and central heating. I ordered a toasted sandwich and a large coffee, and sat back, contented.

The conversation Jayne and I had had about the selkie popped into my mind – a powerful, mystical female, grounded and tethered by a man. I resisted the urge to examine that picture again, and instead, I looked up and ahead to another picture that caught my eye. It was larger, in shades of faded green. To one side, a king and queen were running away, hand in hand, leaving behind a crowd of mythical creatures, diminutive humans, swans, toads, oversized insects. Dark woods loomed in the background, but the fore figures were smiling, the king looking back and down to his queen.

Sophie had said she enjoyed art, too. I suppose there was actually much you might have had in common. That made sense, seeing as Daniel was drawn to you both. Perhaps you could even have been friends. I pictured her, visiting you at your own gallery exhibition. Could Daniel really have told you not to pursue your dream? Thinking about his reaction to Jessica's work, or even to seeing her again, and how he had doted on you, adored you, it seemed unlikely. Perhaps you had used him as an excuse for your own lack of confidence and ambition in the area. Perhaps what Sebastien had said was true, but only his truth, and half of your truth, and so a version of the truth. A version of your life. It seemed to me, there was not one objective Susie that we all shared. There were dozens of versions of you, and your story.

I stood up and leant across the table to read the label on the picture: Oberon and Titania. Oberon and Titania; the king and queen of the fairies. I knew this story, and I searched then, eyes darting in the crowd behind them in the picture until I found him. Bottom the Weaver, with the head of an ass, sitting on the floor in the corner of the image, rejected. Dejected. A fool. It was A Midsummer Night's Dream.

**

I stayed in the tearoom for a couple of hours; cake followed lunch, as it should. I had a second coffee and checked the bus timetable on my phone, enjoying the warmth and the low chatter in the room. The low winter sun had dissolved into cloud and through the window I noted that it started to shower; I paid the bill and was lucky to make it safely onto the last bus home, just before the worst of it had begun.

The steam on the windows and the dull light made for little view, as I journeyed back, contented, clutching a bottle of water, thinking of Jayne, of Nanna and Granny, of Jessica, Sophie, and you.

255

For a large part of the trip, I was the sole occupant of the bus. I sat and scrolled through the photographs on my phone, as I had done so many times before. But this time, I allowed myself to look at the ones of you with Daniel. Smiling, hugging, kissing. Happy.

Chapter 29

The next evening, I was standing on a small stepladder, fitting my new lampshade, when the front doorbell rang. I had wondered if Daniel would visit; it seemed his style to appear with flowers and an apology, or grimacing concern. I suspected it was him – who else would come unannounced? I was right but, for once, I was glad to be so.

As I poured us each some water, he settled on the sofa and I noticed he grabbed a cushion, encircled it with his arms, hugging. It was a fleeting, simple moment from this usually steadfast and secure young man. He dropped the cushion back to his side as I sat down. Perhaps he was nervous. He launched straight into an explanation without introduction. I was glad at his lack of pleasantries.

"I went to school with him – Matt. He's always liked a drink but that was... well."

He shook his head and looked away.

"He's just come through a divorce. His wife has a new man, I understand. He suspects it started before they were completely over; someone was saying the other night. That could just be gossip. Anyway, I don't know..." He trailed away. "That's no excuse, obviously."

Divorce. How was it that your peers were now old enough for divorce? A stream of life events flowed by me within a moment: marriage; children; Christenings; a child leaving home; retirement. All things that were lost to you now. Drowned, sodden. Gone.

"No harm done. It all happened quickly, but thankfully that means it was over quickly, too. At least, not to me. It was your party, though. I hope it didn't completely spoil it?"

He didn't answer.

"Can you believe Soph?" He was shaking his head. "I've never seen her like that before. I should have known she had it in her, but I didn't. Didn't expect that. She's always so... gentle."

"'Though she be but little she is fierce'," I said.

He looked at me; seemed to process the words.

"Yeah, she is. Yes. Some people are, aren't they? They surprise you."

"People constantly surprise me, Daniel," I said.

We sat for a while and chatted about other people that had been at the party, about his parents and his colleagues, his work. He told me about his gifts. Why he had chosen that specific place – they used to go there as a child, at least once a month. It held happy memories for him, he said. He spoke with genuine affection of his father – who had been ill last year, it seemed. It struck me that I was no longer wading through eggshells, tentative, halting when I spoke to him. I was now at ease. I wasn't sure exactly what had changed. But it had. Finally. I hoped it would last.

"One of my oldest friends lives in Dubai, you know. He sent me an amazing gift. An IOU for me and Sophie to visit him. He can get some deal on flights via his company, and he lives in these beautiful, serviced apartments; the pictures are simply stunning... Soph's already been looking up travel arrangements today. We'd need to go soon because—" he stopped and glanced at me.

It struck me again, this feeling, suspicion, but this time the fear had gone.

"It would be better to travel sooner rather than later," he stated.

I nodded.

He thanked me for his gift, and said they planned to go for Sophie's birthday in a couple of months, so it was the perfect present. He finished his water, and then looked to be shuffling himself towards getting ready to go. These were the signs; I knew him well enough to know. He pulled his legs in, sat up straighter and fidgeted with the jacket he had kept on all this time.

"Before I go," he said. "I've got a gift for you. I was up in the attic last week and I came across a box of things, and I thought you might like it. No point in it sitting up there, gathering dust. It's a – well, self-explanatory, really."

He was fiddling with his bag as he spoke, bent over and unzipping it, smoothly. He pulled out a large, spiral bound hard, black book.

"A notebook?" I asked.

"Sketchbook."

He was holding it out to me with two hands, but I was sitting on mine. For some reason, I was reluctant to reach out for it. I was leaning back slightly. Nervous.

He nodded at it.

"Go on," he said. "I think she'd want you to have it."

He was right, of course. You would. I took the book and placed it on my lap without opening it. It felt fragile, somehow. Personal.

Daniel leaned over me and gently prized open the front, like a tender father about to read a bedtime story, or a teacher showing a parent their child's first schoolwork.

"It's just little pictures. Doodles that she did sometimes, of things she planned to paint."

"Preparatory sketches."

He chuckled, "That's the one. Preparatory sketches."

The words sounded clumsy in his mouth.

He was slowly turning pages, revealing charcoal drawings sheathed under tracing paper, full-page drawings of abstract scenes in black pen, delicate still-life pencil sketches. Beautiful. Detailed. Raw. On some pages, whole paragraphs of notes were written in minute block capitals. On others, towards the back of the book, torn scraps of paper had been glued in and folded up. Daniel didn't unfold them; he kept turning pages, a little too fast, now. I could feel the pulse of you in there; I wanted to trace my fingertip down the lines and curves you had etched, to hold the images up close and look deep inside, to step inside, but he was strumming the pages, flicking through, smiling wanly.

He shut the book before we had reached the end, vaguely bored. But then, he had never been very interested in that side of things – and it was a sensitive touch to realise I had, and the book would be better placed with me.

We can't judge others simply for not being the same as us.

"Thank you," I said, rubbing the last rolls of dust off the front of the book. "Thank you so much."

***

After he had gone, I went back to sorting the finishing touches of the hallway. I used screws and rawl plugs to secure Jessica's pictures, terrified that one would fall and be damaged. The framing workshop had done an exceptional job. The pictures looked bold and strong on the wall, and the white frames, white paintwork seemed to illuminate the blue sea and sky, and the little flashes of green from Jessica's dress, tucked away in each of them.

I replaced the photographs I had taken down, wiping clean their frames, and putting them back on the radiator shelf, and then cut the last bloom of agapanthus from the garden, placing it in a clear bottle next to the photos, below the pictures, next to an expensive reed diffuser, with essential oil mimicking a fresh sea scent. I stepped back into the kitchen and then took in the full length of the hall. It was crisp and light. Perfect.

One last touch needed to be made, to finish this scene and make it whole. I went into the kitchen and unhooked the Mother's Day card you had made me, from where it was stuck to the fridge. I had worried I would not find it, but of course it had been under the bed in a box, next to your clothes, and my scrapbook. I gave it one gentle dust and then placed it cautiously within my new frame, with its silver twigs and branches forming a halo around it. Your beautiful sketch of my garden, with its lilies.

The telephone rang, and I glanced at the clock, thinking it must be Jack for his usual Sunday evening call. I was right: it was later than I had realised.

"Mumster!" he cried.

I settled in comfortably on the sofa, in the spot where your boyfriend – ex-boyfriend—had been, just an hour earlier. I picked up the cushion and hugged it myself, as Jack started to chatter away.

Half an hour passed on the phone to Jack. I told him about my handiwork in the hallway and promised to send him some photos. We spent some time planning my forthcoming Christmas shopping trip to see him; I told him about Daniel's party, though spared him the finer details of the incident.

"Oh, and you no longer have to feel desperately guilty that I have days and nights alone over the holiday period without you," I teased. "I've agreed to start volunteering with Jessica."

"The refuge?" he said. "How brilliant."

"It's not a refuge exactly," I corrected. "I'll tell you all about it when I see you."

"Well, whatever it is, I think it's a great idea. You're an untapped well of skills and talent at the moment. And it would be good to have some…

structure and a… a… hobby? I don't know what the word is."

"A new focus," I said.

"A focus," he repeated. "Yes, that's it. We all need one of those."

"Anyway, speaking of hobbies, you will be proud of your darling mother as not only am I taking up volunteering, but I've signed up for a leisure course starting in January."

"Awesome. That's a turn-up for the books. I thought you said evening classes were for losers and oldies?"

"I doubt very much that I would ever have called anyone a loser. Though perhaps I fit in both of those categories, on reflection."

"I'm sure it was something equally disparaging," Jack said. "So, what is it? Latin? Foraging? Taking up floristry?"

"While all of those things do sound quite appealing, Jayne and I have signed up for an art class. Sketching. One of Susie's old friends is going to be the tutor, and when she told me about it at Daniel's party, I thought it could be just the thing I needed."

"Wow. Good for you. I wish I was that brave."

Brave. Was I?

"Oh, and funny thing… You'll never guess what Daniel dropped off today. Susie's sketchbook. One of her drawing pads. I've only looked quickly but I'd best be careful as even a cursory glance shows me how lacking in skills I am, compared to her."

"A sketchbook? Why?" Jack asked, confused.

263

"He said he found it in the attic and thought I might want it. It's stuffed full of her work. To be honest, I think he wanted rid of it but didn't have the gall to throw it away. I know that feeling. I still have things I must sort through, one day. It's hard to know what to do with them."

"Blimey. So now you have one more thing of hers? But actually, that is thoughtful."

"Yes, yes, it is. But he is, though. Isn't he?... Well, the sketchbook, it's almost full. Just a few blank pages near the end. I think it might even be the last one she was working in. I'll be able to figure it out – she's dated some of the work, I think. And there are leaflets, and scraps of paper folded up neatly and stuck in. Her ideas. I can bring it up with me when I come to see you if you like?"

"Yes, of course. I would love to see that... But mum, listen, it won't upset you, will it? Looking at all that stuff? Her handwriting and everything?"

I could hear the old anxiety in his voice.

"No, darling. It's very tiring being sad or worried all the time," I said and realised it was true.

I had been trying my hardest not to let irrational thoughts run away with me, but I had been stretched to the limit, these last few months.

"I think it's time I put my energy into other things, don't you?"

She waited a few moments after he shut the bathroom door;
stood still, silent, next to the handle. She kept her breath tight
and small. He had scattered his flip-flops in a stagger as if
they could run away, and she noticed he had left his mobile
phone in the room. This was not like him. He had just told
her to check the time. And then he had left his mobile phone
in the room. In the room. With her.

Was it unlocked? Was the camera on? No. It wouldn't
be. Don't be silly.

But she didn't risk touching it.

He would have been furious.

The shower started, and the sound of the water's high-
pressure needled her skin. She could feel it. Her body was
starting to tremor.

She imagined the bridge of his nose, the filaments of bristle
on his upper lip as he lifted his beautiful face into the shards
of water. This was too much. She leapt away from the door,
taking two steps further into the hotel room as she turned,
twisting in a delicate pirouette.

Her bare feet tapped along the tiles as she scampered
towards the balcony. She could still hear the shower but didn't
dare look back as she yanked the sliding doors open, enough
to squeeze through.

She saw her forearm, burnt pink, hairs withered and
frazzled, skin cracked and dry. Rawhide. Unattractive.

No: ugly.

The air drowned her face in heat, dissolving the chill of the
air-conditioning in a second, though there was a touch of the
breeze she craved. She was on the other side, one hand
stretching and curling around the latch to shut it behind her,

gently. Quietly. He must not hear. He had told her to go to bed.

Tired. She was tired. But bed would not help. It was getting too hard. She could feel her head, her bones, hollow, insubstantial as a wren's egg. The familiar dizziness was there – each time she moved her head too quickly, her vision swam, and the floor lifted and undulated. Sometimes she thought this was good – if she was hungry and raw, she was using up calories. Burning up fat. But other times she was weak-willed and wanted to give in – she considered eating, alone. She fantasised about breads and cakes and cheese and puddings. She contemplated hiding in cupboards, or the bathroom, with mounds of carbohydrates.

Daniel would be so disappointed in her: she imagined he could see it around her, as an aura, or a swathe. As if he could see her thoughts about her. That he would know what she was thinking.

That she was going to give up.

She had a problem with food: eating far too much when he met her. He was helping her. He was the only one she could trust.

Her vision was encircled in black, momentarily, swooping in from the outside to the centre. She was staggering backwards, now, losing her footing, shaking, shuddering. Staggering backwards and so she clenched her right hand onto her left wrist. If she held it tight enough maybe she could stop the tremor in her bones. But her left leg tripped around her right – stupid enough to fall over nothing. Stupid. Fool. She was pinned, entangled in herself – and she pictured chickens strung up in the market, ham hocks on chains and hooks.

Carefully, she edged baby steps until she was up against the low, tiled wall of the balcony. She turned around. The floor

266

was warm, but then she felt the back of her heels against the cool surface, the feeling creeping up her legs, her hips, as she pushed further against the short wall.

She was at the edge. Her arms and hands and fingers were a confused tangle of limbs, over and under like a ball of wool, pushing in a mass against her chest and gullet as she turned them around and around. Like she wasn't in control of her own body. Agitated. Twitching, internally.

She tried to still herself; to calm herself. But she could not.

She needed him. It was true. She almost cried for him, almost, but kept the words in her throat. Who could tell how he would react? She wasn't able to judge, anymore. So, it was better to be quiet. It was confusing. Exhausting.

The wall was a comfort, but she still felt she could not breathe. She turned, face in the breeze, gulping, and caught a familiar figure from the corner of her eye. He had come out onto his balcony in the next block and gone in again. Wet trunks now hung and dripped from the broken drying rail.

She called out to him, though she knew it was futile. Nervous to shout too loudly; she might have been heard over the sound of the shower and she should be in bed. She should be asleep.

Plus, it wasn't right to spend time talking to Sebastien, no. He couldn't be trusted. And Jessica, even. They were not good for her. They were whores.

What are they, Susie?

But that didn't seem right.

They had argued. Last night. Argued like they had never done before. Rowed throughout the night a dozen times before they had ever said a word: in looks, frowns, sighs. She felt unlike herself, emboldened by the holiday, the sun, her friends she supposed. And she thought this would be imperceptible to everyone else. A hidden dance between them. But no, when they got back to the room, he had explained, calmly, that everyone knew. Even the waiter could see: didn't she notice the way he stared at her? He kept talking to her? They could all see what she was like, with her anger and her food, and always picking a fight. Always just a little bit paranoid. They could all see.

That's why they didn't want to sit with her. That's why they would stay by the pool, stay away, sit away, look away, and think about what you are saying, Susie.

Really think about it.

He had explained it plainly. She was upset. But if she thought about it, truly thought about it, calmly, it was illogical to be angry with him. Who should she trust? These dippy, artsy friends? Or the man who loved her? She didn't need them anyway. They certainly didn't care about her. Even her mum didn't care.

I'm sorry. I know it hurts. I know.

Her mum cared about nothing but her bloody garden, he said. Or the ridiculous birds she fed. Those precious birds. She'd be more upset if something happened to those big blue flowers of hers than if something happened to one of us. Imagine that? If someone was to do something to those stupid fucking flowers? Ha! He'd love to see her face.

The bitch.

But no. That couldn't be right.

She grabbed at her clothes as they got in the way. Ropes. Tight. Hot. She wanted them off. Too many layers. And she wore her shame like a shroud. Its blackness jumbled with the fabric of her clothes, her soul, her voice, and she could not breathe. She did not cry.

268

She leant forward, her body arching steeply over the edge of the balcony. She felt the breeze hit the back of her neck, cool and real. Beautiful. No need to be scared. This was the scene she had drawn in her sketchbook, earlier. That damn sketchbook that she carried everywhere.

It's a waste of time, Susie. Put it away.

What a load of shit.

But no, this was the only thing he said that she was sure he was wrong about. She was certain. In her little book, she drew lines and circles and shapes, and she felt free. Calm. Herself. It was her space, her place. An honest place and time where she was wholly absorbed and could draw what she wanted. Write what she wanted. And she did. She had written it all. Everything.

Everything.

In the only place she could be sure he would never look.

She put her hands onto the wall of the balcony and pulled her legs up until she was a curled beetle. Then she pushed herself onto her knees. The breeze hit her shoulders, her upper arms. It tried to lift the skirt of her dress. It lifted her.

She pushed herself up with one hand. Rising, unfolding, she could feel it. Yes. Her body danced on the wall. Danced in the breeze.

Lifting. Rising. Flying.

Free.

She made her decision.

And then she jumped.

Acknowledgements

Thank you for reading my book. If you have enjoyed it, please leave me a review. You have no idea the difference this can make.

Thank you also to my early readers, including (of course) the lovely Stuart. P.S. No, it's not about you.

About the Author

Dreena Collins lives in the Channel Isles, where she works in a mental health education charity. She has been published online and within collections, including the Bath Flash Fiction Award and Reflex Press anthologies. She has been listed and placed in several writing competitions, such as The Bridport Prize (shortlisted) and Flash 500 (first place).

Dreena has published several short story and flash fiction collections, including Bird Wing, which was shortlisted in the SPR Book Awards for 2020, and She Had Met Liars Before, shortlisted in the Chanticleer Awards of 2021.

She is a social media geek. Find more of her work (and wordy memes and quotes) at any of the following:

Website: http://dreenawriting.co.uk
Facebook: dreenawriting
Instagram: dreenawriting
Twitter: @dreenac

ALSO BY

Dreena Collins
Literary short stories

Embers (Tales of Courage and Comeuppance)

She Had Met Liars Before: Six Very Short Stories of Strength and Survival

Taste: Six of the Best (Six Readers' Favourites from previous works)

Collected (The Complete Stories: The Blue Hour Series plus Bird Wing)

Bird Wing (A Flash Fiction Collection)

The Day I Nearly Drowned (Short Stories Vol. Two)

The Blue Hour (Short Stories Vol. One)

After something different? Dreena also writes contemporary genre fiction under **Jane Harvey,** *in The Hummingbird House series.*

The Landlord of Hummingbird House (Book One)

Buttercups in the Basement (Book Two)

Searching For Sandra (Book Three, a novella)

Turn over for an extract from Book One.

Chapter One:
April

He was sitting on the wall outside the house. Not at all like she had expected. His grey t-shirt was distressed and raw-edged, the short sleeves taut around his biceps. The sharp point of a black tattoo poked out from beneath the fabric on his left arm.

He was poised, still, hands clasped together as he stared straight ahead.

April parked as close as she could, her little Fiat squeezing neatly into the last remaining space on that side of the street. She got out, grabbing her phone and keys but leaving behind the Tetris stack of boxes and bags that filled the car.

As she walked towards him, he didn't move even though he must have heard her approaching. It was peculiar, really. She couldn't put her finger on what else it was that seemed so odd. But there was something majestic about him. So centred and still.

He wasn't playing with a phone, she realised, with a jolt.

"Hi!" she called when she was just a couple of metres away.

He turned his head towards her but kept the rest of his body still. He had stubble, but not a full beard, thankfully. Why these men insisted on hiding their jaws with beards was a mystery to her.

Printed in Great Britain
by Amazon

12793241R00162